NEVER

LIVE

(A May Moore Suspense Thriller —Book Three)

BLAKE PIERCE

Blake Pierce

Blake Pierce is the USA Today bestselling author of the RILEY PAGE mystery series, which includes seventeen books. Blake Pierce is also the author of the MACKENZIE WHITE mystery series, comprising fourteen books; of the AVERY BLACK mystery series, comprising six books; of the KERI LOCKE mystery series, comprising five books; of the MAKING OF RILEY PAIGE mystery series, comprising six books; of the KATE WISE mystery series, comprising seven books; of the CHLOE FINE psychological suspense mystery, comprising six books; of the JESSE HUNT psychological suspense thriller series, comprising twenty four books; of the AU PAIR psychological suspense thriller series, comprising three books; of the ZOE PRIME mystery series, comprising six books; of the ADELE SHARP mystery series, comprising fifteen books, of the EUROPEAN VOYAGE cozy mystery series, comprising four books; of the new LAURA FROST FBI suspense thriller, comprising nine books (and counting); of the new ELLA DARK FBI suspense thriller, comprising eleven books (and counting); of the A YEAR IN EUROPE cozy mystery series, comprising nine books, of the AVA GOLD mystery series, comprising six books (and counting); of the RACHEL GIFT mystery series, comprising eight books (and counting); of the VALERIE LAW mystery series, comprising nine books (and counting); of the PAIGE KING mystery series, comprising six books (and counting); of the MAY MOORE mystery series, comprising six books (and counting); and the CORA SHIELDS mystery series, comprising three books (and counting).

An avid reader and lifelong fan of the mystery and thriller genres, Blake loves to hear from you, so please feel free to visit www.blakepierceauthor.com to learn more and stay in touch.

BOOKS BY BLAKE PIERCE

CORA SHIELDS MYSTERY SERIES
UNDONE (Book #1)
UNWANTED (Book #2)
UNHINGED (Book #3)

MAY MOORE SUSPENSE THRILLER
NEVER RUN (Book #1)
NEVER TELL (Book #2)
NEVER LIVE (Book #3)
NEVER HIDE (Book #4)
NEVER FORGIVE (Book #5)
NEVER AGAIN (Book #6)

PAIGE KING MYSTERY SERIES
THE GIRL HE PINED (Book #1)
THE GIRL HE CHOSE (Book #2)
THE GIRL HE TOOK (Book #3)
THE GIRL HE WISHED (Book #4)
THE GIRL HE CROWNED (Book #5)
THE GIRL HE WATCHED (Book #6)

VALERIE LAW MYSTERY SERIES
NO MERCY (Book #1)
NO PITY (Book #2)
NO FEAR (Book #3)
NO SLEEP (Book #4)
NO QUARTER (Book #5)
NO CHANCE (Book #6)
NO REFUGE (Book #7)
NO GRACE (Book #8)
NO ESCAPE (Book #9)

RACHEL GIFT MYSTERY SERIES
HER LAST WISH (Book #1)
HER LAST CHANCE (Book #2)

HER LAST HOPE (Book #3)
HER LAST FEAR (Book #4)
HER LAST CHOICE (Book #5)
HER LAST BREATH (Book #6)
HER LAST MISTAKE (Book #7)
HER LAST DESIRE (Book #8)

AVA GOLD MYSTERY SERIES
CITY OF PREY (Book #1)
CITY OF FEAR (Book #2)
CITY OF BONES (Book #3)
CITY OF GHOSTS (Book #4)
CITY OF DEATH (Book #5)
CITY OF VICE (Book #6)

A YEAR IN EUROPE
A MURDER IN PARIS (Book #1)
DEATH IN FLORENCE (Book #2)
VENGEANCE IN VIENNA (Book #3)
A FATALITY IN SPAIN (Book #4)

ELLA DARK FBI SUSPENSE THRILLER
GIRL, ALONE (Book #1)
GIRL, TAKEN (Book #2)
GIRL, HUNTED (Book #3)
GIRL, SILENCED (Book #4)
GIRL, VANISHED (Book 5)
GIRL ERASED (Book #6)
GIRL, FORSAKEN (Book #7)
GIRL, TRAPPED (Book #8)
GIRL, EXPENDABLE (Book #9)
GIRL, ESCAPED (Book #10)
GIRL, HIS (Book #11)

LAURA FROST FBI SUSPENSE THRILLER
ALREADY GONE (Book #1)
ALREADY SEEN (Book #2)
ALREADY TRAPPED (Book #3)
ALREADY MISSING (Book #4)
ALREADY DEAD (Book #5)

ALREADY TAKEN (Book #6)
ALREADY CHOSEN (Book #7)
ALREADY LOST (Book #8)
ALREADY HIS (Book #9)

EUROPEAN VOYAGE COZY MYSTERY SERIES
MURDER (AND BAKLAVA) (Book #1)
DEATH (AND APPLE STRUDEL) (Book #2)
CRIME (AND LAGER) (Book #3)
MISFORTUNE (AND GOUDA) (Book #4)
CALAMITY (AND A DANISH) (Book #5)
MAYHEM (AND HERRING) (Book #6)

ADELE SHARP MYSTERY SERIES
LEFT TO DIE (Book #1)
LEFT TO RUN (Book #2)
LEFT TO HIDE (Book #3)
LEFT TO KILL (Book #4)
LEFT TO MURDER (Book #5)
LEFT TO ENVY (Book #6)
LEFT TO LAPSE (Book #7)
LEFT TO VANISH (Book #8)
LEFT TO HUNT (Book #9)
LEFT TO FEAR (Book #10)
LEFT TO PREY (Book #11)
LEFT TO LURE (Book #12)
LEFT TO CRAVE (Book #13)
LEFT TO LOATHE (Book #14)
LEFT TO HARM (Book #15)

THE AU PAIR SERIES
ALMOST GONE (Book#1)
ALMOST LOST (Book #2)
ALMOST DEAD (Book #3)

ZOE PRIME MYSTERY SERIES
FACE OF DEATH (Book#1)
FACE OF MURDER (Book #2)
FACE OF FEAR (Book #3)
FACE OF MADNESS (Book #4)

IF SHE SAW (Book #2)
IF SHE RAN (Book #3)
IF SHE HID (Book #4)
IF SHE FLED (Book #5)
IF SHE FEARED (Book #6)
IF SHE HEARD (Book #7)

THE MAKING OF RILEY PAIGE SERIES
WATCHING (Book #1)
WAITING (Book #2)
LURING (Book #3)
TAKING (Book #4)
STALKING (Book #5)
KILLING (Book #6)

RILEY PAIGE MYSTERY SERIES
ONCE GONE (Book #1)
ONCE TAKEN (Book #2)
ONCE CRAVED (Book #3)
ONCE LURED (Book #4)
ONCE HUNTED (Book #5)
ONCE PINED (Book #6)
ONCE FORSAKEN (Book #7)
ONCE COLD (Book #8)
ONCE STALKED (Book #9)
ONCE LOST (Book #10)
ONCE BURIED (Book #11)
ONCE BOUND (Book #12)
ONCE TRAPPED (Book #13)
ONCE DORMANT (Book #14)
ONCE SHUNNED (Book #15)
ONCE MISSED (Book #16)
ONCE CHOSEN (Book #17)

MACKENZIE WHITE MYSTERY SERIES
BEFORE HE KILLS (Book #1)
BEFORE HE SEES (Book #2)
BEFORE HE COVETS (Book #3)
BEFORE HE TAKES (Book #4)
BEFORE HE NEEDS (Book #5)

PROLOGUE

Giggling, holding onto Dylan's hand, Alyssa stumbled along the trail that led into the woods. Behind them, the raucous sounds of the post-prom party echoed in the summer night.

Alyssa heard laughter, drunken yells, the throb of music from the loudspeakers set up in the lakeside pavilion. Smoke and sparks from the bonfire wafted into the air.

Ahead of them, the woods were cool. Green leaves rustled. A tree root nearly tripped Alyssa up. She clung onto Dylan, shrieking with laughter, glad of the excuse to hold tighter onto his wiry, muscular arm.

"Not so fast! I nearly fell over," she warned.

"Hey, sorry! You okay?" he asked, sliding his other arm around her.

"I'm okay," she whispered, snuggling into him. He had taken off the dress shirt he'd worn for the prom itself. Now, he was in a white T-shirt that was so thin she could feel the hard planes of his chest through it.

"Not too cold?" he murmured, and his breath warmed the nape of her neck.

"Not too cold now." She giggled again.

She was drunk, but she knew what she wanted. She knew what she'd been hoping for, since she'd seen that smoldering look on his face, when he'd danced with her at the prom. How breathless she'd felt when he'd whispered in her ear.

And now was the time.

He turned and kissed her, and Alyssa felt swept off her feet by the headiness of lust.

"You're so hot, Alyssa," Dylan said, and his voice was a little huskier than it had been before. His lips brushed her cheek.

Alyssa's heart hammered loudly against her chest. She'd known him since they were in kindergarten, but it seemed right that they were together now. They belonged together; she was sure of it. It was meant to be.

Dylan broke off the kiss and downed his beer.

"How about we sit here a while?" he suggested.

They'd gone further into the woods than Alyssa had realized. The party sounds had faded.

Now, there was a mossy smell that Alyssa didn't like. It was kind of damp, with an undertone of old, rotting leaves.

Dylan, as he slid down with his back to a tree, didn't seem to notice.

But drunk as Alyssa was, she didn't feel the same way as he grasped her waist, lowering her down beside him.

Her dress was too short for this. There were sticks and stones under the moldy leaves, and they were scouring her skin.

She didn't know how far she should go with Dylan. She really, really liked him. But she knew he had a reputation as a class stud. She didn't want him to dump her afterward. She knew he'd done that with other girls. It would be so humiliating if he talked about it to his friends, and laughed that she'd just been a one-night stand for him.

But had he looked at the other girls in the same way? With that melting expression in his dark eyes that made desire flare inside her?

"You're so special," he murmured. Now his hands were on her, easing their way up her legs, teasing open the zipper in the front of her dress.

It was wonderful, but it was terrifying, and her parents would be furious; and although drunk, Alyssa realized she wasn't drunk enough.

She suddenly didn't know if she was ready for this.

"Look, I'm not comfortable here," Alyssa began, fearing her words would shatter the moment and break the magical attraction between them. If this was serious, she didn't want to mess it up now.

"Why? What's wrong?" Now his voice was sharper. She could tell he was pissed at her refusal to go along with things.

"I - uh - "

She wasn't sure how to voice her unease. Probably she shouldn't say that she was now thinking about how mad her folks would be.

"I'm not comfortable on the ground here. I'm - I'm worried about bugs. And ticks."

"Ticks?" Sounding incredulous, Dylan spluttered with laughter. "I don't think there are any ticks here. But I'll - I'll tell you what." He leaned closer. "My car's parked close to the pavilion, so I'll run back and go get us a blanket."

"Okay," Alyssa said.

That wasn't what she'd intended. She'd intended for them to both go back, to buy her some time. But now, Dylan had scrambled to his feet and was loping back in the direction of the pavilion.

Alyssa sat uneasily on the leaves. She was now feeling very aware that the zipper of her dress was too far down, the skirt had been pushed up to her thighs, and she was now alone. As she sat, she tried to think

2

through the logistics of all of this. He would come back with a blanket. But that would kind of pressure her to go along with things from there. She'd feel that she'd somehow agreed to whatever would follow, if he brought a blanket back. That action would be sealing the deal. She'd find it harder to say no.

"But I don't think I can," Alyssa muttered, to the forest around her. "I'm still not sure."

He'd been a great kisser, though. She wouldn't mind another kiss.

Alyssa thought again about that kiss, and it made her feel better, but she couldn't get the knot of discomfort out of her mind. Something, somehow, was feeling not right here and she didn't know why.

It didn't make sense. She tried her best to work out what it was.

It didn't help that the woods felt too dark. Too remote. Reality was pushing its way through the haze of alcohol and hormones that dominated Alyssa's current mindset.

She was alone in the woods without Dylan, and she was drunk.

Then a twig snapped, and Alyssa's head turned sharply. She felt a flare of fear. She'd sensed someone behind her. Or something. Was an animal creeping up?

Twisting around, she stared apprehensively through the darkened lattice of branches and leaves. And her eyes widened as she saw something. Or rather, someone.

Suddenly, she realized what was going down and why this shadowy figure was lurking here. Someone, a guy from the looks of things, had snuck up in the woods. Perhaps they'd come this way to take a pee, but had then stayed to watch what she and Dylan would be getting up to.

That was sick!

Alyssa's trickle of fear was shoved aside by a torrent of righteous anger.

"Get out of here, perv!" she yelled, drawing herself to her knees, hastily yanking up her zipper as she glowered at him.

She had expected the guy to hotfoot it after that warning, knowing that she'd seen him and that if he stuck around, she'd work out who it was and tell everyone.

But he didn't turn and run off like she'd expected.

Instead, he paced closer, his footsteps crunching over the path. A shaft of moonlight speared through the darkness of the canopy and then Alyssa saw his face.

She stared at him in absolute shock.

"Wait! *You?* What are you doing here? What the - ?"

Her irate question turned to a scream as the man lunged forward.

3

Alyssa scrambled to her feet.

This was no peeping Tom scenario. Too late, she realized this was something different. Something deadlier. It wasn't only the fact he was looking to grab her. It was the expression in his face that she could now see as he neared her. In his eyes. There was an evil anticipation there that chilled her blood.

She whirled around, shocked and panicked, and began to run. Away from him, which meant deeper into the woods. But her high-heeled sandals were not the right shoes for speed.

Her chest was tight with fear and she felt as if she was choking. Her ankle twisted on a rock, invisible in the dark, and she let out a gasp of pain.

He was behind her. She could hear the footsteps getting closer. Thud, thud, thud.

She was drunk. She was going the wrong way. Deeper into the woods. Further away from anyone who could help.

She staggered, screaming again, wishing Dylan would come back, praying that he'd somehow arrive in time, because she'd never imagined this could happen. That she'd be chased through the woods. By someone she knew and trusted, who had turned into a terrifying monster.

But there were only the footsteps. Just one set. Thud, thud.

And then, he grabbed her shoulders. Iron-hard fingers gripped her, tugging her back to him.

"No!" Alyssa screamed again, but those strong hands had found her neck.

"No! No!" she shrieked, flailing.

But then the fingers closed hard around her throat. Her words choked in her mouth.

These strong fingers were killing her. Her head felt dizzy, and she felt as if she was floating, even as the shadows closed in upon her.

Alyssa tried to scream once more, but her voice had been stolen.

Instead, she slipped into darkness.

CHAPTER ONE

"You'll never find your sister." The voice whispering in May Moore's ear was sibilant, threatening. "And you'd better not start looking. Because if you do, I'll find you. Then you'll be sorry."

With a gasp, May woke from her nightmare, sitting bolt upright in bed, breathing hard. Shivers prickled her spine. She reached for the light switch, needing to banish the shadows that seemed to be lurking in her quiet bedroom.

That had been a weird and troubling dream. How had her subconscious come up with such a scenario? she wondered. Her dreams had definitely been more intense since she'd reopened her sister's missing person case. It was preoccupying her more than she realized.

Looking at the clock, she saw it was four a.m. It was Sunday morning, the one day when she could usually sleep in, if the responsibilities of her job as the county's deputy allowed. But she knew she wouldn't get back to sleep now.

Instead, May got up, pulling on jeans and a T-shirt, and sat down at the kitchen table. In another half-hour it would start getting light, revealing the summer-green view of farmland that the kitchen window offered.

In the meantime, she decided to spend some more time analyzing the evidence and file in front of her.

The disappearance of her sister, Lauren, ten years ago had shattered May's life. She'd agonized over how it was possible, in the calm town of Fairshore, Tamarack County, Minnesota, that someone could disappear without a trace.

She thought in a way that Lauren's disappearance had pushed both her and her older sister Kerry into an investigation career. High-flying Kerry, always the more successful sister, had aced the entrance exams and joined the FBI. To her shame, May had missed the mark by a couple of critical points and had become a local police detective. Her recent promotion to the first female county deputy was something she was proud of, but she knew that to her parents, Kerry would always be the one who had truly achieved in life.

However, two recent cases in her own neighborhood had proved to May that murder was truly everywhere, and that small town folk could be well concealed psychopaths. This was why she was relooking at Lauren's case with a new passion, keen to bring her new experience to this old investigation and see if anything had been left unexplored.

There were only a few items of evidence that had been found on the shores of Eagle Lake. With the case reopened, May had been able to investigate the evidence box.

It contained a water bottle. A button from Lauren's shirtsleeve. A scrap of bloody fabric linked to Lauren's top. And a small key, with a label that had, so far, been beyond May's efforts to decipher.

She had no idea what this key was for. She hadn't known about it. It hadn't been listed in the evidence log, or mentioned in the police report.

"Why was it there?" May muttered to herself, staring at the darkened window as she took a sip of her coffee.

She wished she could ask the previous sheriff who'd managed the county, and the investigation, at the time. But he'd passed away from a heart attack a couple of years ago. Sheriff Jack, the new county sheriff who was May's boss, hadn't been involved in that case at all.

"What does it open?"

Yet again, she turned the key around and around in her hands. Sheriff Jack had given her permission to bring the evidence box home at night, because May hadn't wanted to work on this case during office hours. Her working day was too busy. She wanted to devote her own time to this case.

May felt compelled to turn over every stone, to sift through the evidence with fresh eyes, and to find out everything she could. She longed to discover something that would help in her personal quest to get answers about her sister's death.

But so far, her spare time was being spent in a state of curiosity and frustration.

She pushed a lock of sandy blonde hair back from her face with a sigh.

She had no idea what the key unlocked, and she couldn't read the label. The lettering was just too smudged. May was wondering if there was some kind of a computer program that might be able to decipher the blurred letters.

She'd researched the type of key, but there were too many possibilities. It wasn't a safe key, that she knew. But it might be a padlock key, a locker key, or maybe a key to another kind of container.

"What did you lock away, Lauren? Where did you go?" May asked the question aloud. Her words felt empty in the stillness of the room.

Sitting at the table, staring at that evidence, she agonized over all the questions that she still had about the day her sister had vanished.

If only she could ask someone, anyone, even all these years later, what had really happened.

She felt terribly guilty that Lauren had walked out after a fight with her. The two sisters had a screaming match about something irrelevant that May couldn't even remember now. She had never been able to get rid of the thought that Lauren's disappearance was her fault. The fight was the reason her sister had stormed out of the house and taken the hiking trail leading to the lake.

And she'd never come back.

Now, May wished she could have apologized for that fight. She missed her sister so much. That day was the last time anyone had seen Lauren.

Except perhaps the person who'd killed her, May thought.

Or was she still alive? Since her body had never been found, May always kept that hope in her heart. She found herself thinking more and more of Lauren recently, especially since Kerry had gotten engaged.

Having her older sister on the way to getting married had caused family to be top of mind for May. Especially since she was going to be involved in organizing this wedding, whether she liked it or not. And that brought a whole new layer of stress to her life at this time.

May knew it would end up being a dream wedding. A fairytale wedding, to a super-successful high-flying lawyer. Being Kerry, her sister was already starting to get into the details of the wedding which would take place the following spring, somewhere in the vicinity of Fairfield.

Also being Kerry, she was already delegating the demanding job of organizing these details to her immediate family, i.e., May. May had already been inundated with questions and 'small favors' over the past week. She feared bigger ones were to come.

Her biggest fear was that Kerry would ask her to be the maid of honor. Thrilled as May would be to stand at her sister's side for this momentous occasion, she knew that being a maid of honor would be like having a full-time job for a number of months.

She would have to take leave from work to cope with the demands on her time this would involve as the wedding drew closer. And she couldn't take leave from work! She, too, had a job that was getting much busier after her promotion. There was a whole different level of responsibility she now had to shoulder, and many new aspects of the job that she was still learning.

May was dreading being put in the situation where she might have to choose between family loyalty and work ethics. It would be terrible if she was forced to choose between hurting her sister and causing a family conflict by saying no, or compromising the job she was so passionate about by agreeing to be the maid of honor. She was looking forward to attending the wedding. What an occasion it would be. She was sure she'd cry buckets of joy when Kerry walked down the aisle to stand next to her handsome, caring fiancé. But the preparations brought a whole level of complexity and expectations that was already threatening to split May's head apart.

Deep down, she sincerely hoped that Kerry would ask someone else who had more free time.

At that moment, her phone rang, jolting her focus back to the present moment.

Immediately, the sound prickled her instincts because a call at this hour was never going to be good news. It could only mean that somewhere out in Tamarack County, a serious crime had been committed.

She snatched up her phone from the table so quickly that she sloshed her coffee over her hand. Frowning, she swiped at the liquid with a paper towel as she glanced at the screen.

Sheriff Jack's name appeared.

May answered the call without hesitation.

"Good morning, Sheriff Jack," she spoke crisply. Even in the early hours of the morning, Jack deserved nothing less than her full professionalism and courtesy.

"Deputy May. Good morning. Sorry for the early call."

She could already hear that her boss sounded worried. May jumped to her feet.

"What's happened?" she asked.

His voice was heavy as he gave her the bad news.

"There's been a serious incident called in. A female student has been killed at the post-prom celebration near the Hazelwood Pavilion."

May drew in a shocked breath.

The Hazelwood Pavilion was a community center near the lake, a few miles outside of Fairshore. This was disturbingly close to home.

She felt horrified that another death had occurred near this lake. They'd dealt with two serious murder cases in the vicinity of Eagle Lake recently. Now, tragedy had struck here again.

As she rushed over to the door to put on her shoes, May asked, "How is this related to the post-prom party? Did you get any details on this death?"

In the back of her mind, she was hoping that it had been an accidental death. Terrible as any death was, at least a drowning or an unlucky fall would not mean that someone had deliberately taken someone else's life.

"The initial call only just came through and I'm still on my way to the scene, so I don't know more. Accounts were confused, but from the report, it seems a woman has turned up dead in the woods behind the pavilion. It didn't seem accidental, from the call-out, but we won't know until we get there."

"A murder?" May asked, alarmed. Her heart was thudding faster, her pulse pounded in her wrists and temples.

"One of the students, I believe." Jack's tone was heavy with worry.

"I'll be there as soon as I can," May promised.

She felt scared at what might be waiting there, and anxious about all the unknown factors.

She cut the call, and quickly put on her jacket, finishing off with her gun belt and her hat.

Fortunately, being so close to home, May knew where the Hazelwood Pavilion was, and didn't need to look at her map as she hurried out of the cottage and jumped into her car.

Minutes later, she was driving in the predawn light to the community center.

Whatever had played out there, it had left a student dead and a family bereaved. If it had not been accidental, someone had to answer for this crime.

And if it had been murder, May knew it would be up to her to find out who had committed this crime, and hunt the killer down.

She felt pressured to get there as fast as she could and start piecing together what had happened.

CHAPTER TWO

By the time May reached the lake, it was fully light on what promised to be a cloudless summer day. She was barely aware of the scenic surroundings as she powered into the Hazelwood Pavilion parking lot, stopping in between Sheriff Jack's cruiser and the car of her investigation partner, Deputy Owen Lovell.

She jumped out, hurrying over the neatly mown grass, following the narrow, paved pathway that wound its way down to the scenic pavilion, with its green roof and white-painted walls, and lavender and rose bushes in planters nearby.

Anxiety flared inside her as she heard the crackle of police radios. It was a terrible thing to see the aftermath of a party that was supposed to be a happy, festive occasion but which had imploded into disaster.

Parents were arriving, looking red-eyed and anxious-faced. "What happened?" she heard them asking each other. "Was this an accident? Was there a fight?"

Knots of people stood around, glancing in the direction of the woods. Girls were sobbing. Boys were standing with their heads bowed, pale and shocked.

The pavilion was decorated with colorful bunting, flapping in the early morning breeze, but to May, the litter of bottles and cans told a different story. Things seemed to have gotten a little out of hand at this post-prom celebration.

She knew with a lurch of her stomach that this would make it harder to probe for the truth.

At that moment, another car pulled up behind May. It was one of the sergeants from the Fairfield police department.

"Hi, Kevin," May greeted him. She glanced around, taking the opportunity to manage the scene before heading to where the body was.

"Could you please wait here, by the parking lot entrance? I don't think anyone should be allowed to leave until we've established more. We may need some on-the-spot witness reports. You can start taking down names and contact details."

"I'll do that," he promised, heading to the open gate and stationing himself there.

May walked the other way, heading to the path leading down to the woods, following the crackles of the radio. Now she could make out the voices of officers and detectives, calling out to each other.

May hurried along the main trail, and then veered off it along a side path toward where the others were, her feet crunching on twigs and grass, stepping over tree roots and around bushes. It was difficult to see the narrow path through the undergrowth, and she had to watch her step carefully to avoid tripping.

As she approached, a tall, dark-haired man turned around and saw her.

"Morning, Owen," she greeted her investigation partner. He looked serious and worried. He was wearing foot covers and gloves.

"Morning, May. I got here a few minutes ago. I can't believe this has happened. At a post-prom party, too."

Owen looked horrified. May saw that he, like her, was deeply troubled by this disaster. Owen had been her partner for a year and had joined the police because he wanted to make a difference in the community.

"We need to find out exactly what happened," she said to him worriedly, and he nodded in agreement.

But, as she approached the body, May's attention was sidetracked by activity in a clearing nearby.

Two paramedics were attending to a young, good-looking man. He was sobbing brokenly and the front of his white shirt was spattered and smeared with blood.

Sheriff Jack was standing by them, watching and waiting, running a hand over his graying hair with a stern expression on his face. He was speaking on the phone. Perhaps he was calling this man's parents, May wondered.

She felt as if she was walking into a complex puzzle, with many different and fragmented pieces. There were some that she didn't know or understand yet. But she knew that everything she was seeing so far would be important. Who was this young man; why was he spattered in blood; had he committed the crime?

There was no time to find out more from Sheriff Jack, because she wanted to move forward and view the body. Even though this scene was out in the woods, May hoped that there might be trace evidence that would help give them clarity. Just as Owen had done, May put on the foot covers and gloves from the cardboard box before approaching any closer.

Then, pressing her lips together firmly, May stepped nearer to where the pathologist was working. It was the county pathologist, Andy Baker, a man she knew well. His eyes were serious over his mask as he glanced around at her and gave a small nod of greeting.

Beyond him, she saw a young woman, lying in the early morning light, staring sightlessly up at the sky, wearing a silver prom dress.

The sight was a horrifying one for May, all the more so because it brought the memories of her sister flooding back. She closed her eyes, feeling a rush of sympathy for this girl and her family. She'd had a life ahead of her, and now it was over.

She had to keep strong and be professional, May resolved. She had to think clearly and be calm, to see and recall every detail.

Looking down, she saw the girl's face was framed by long, luxurious curls. Her eyes were closed and her skin was pale, ashen. Her lips were parted. Her makeup was smudged. She was surrounded by red petals, that now looked wilted and drooped. They were scattered around her body, with one or two lying on her dress.

Rose petals? Had they been scattered there after the crime? That was very strange, May thought. And it was a crime. The cause of death was clearly visible. May didn't even need the coroner who was examining the body to explain what she saw. She gasped as she stared at the visible evidence.

She had been strangled. The marks on her neck and the evidence in her face, including a nosebleed staining her face and dress, told the story of the violent scene that had played out in these peaceful woods.

Strangulation. The word felt wrong, impossible, as May stared at the corpse. How could anyone have done such a thing? What had played out?

Had it been a crime of passion? she wondered. Fueled by excessive drink and emotion, had someone committed this violent act in the heat of the moment?

Or had it happened some other way?

A prickle of fear danced along the back of her neck, almost like someone was watching her. But when she turned to look, she could see nothing out of the ordinary. Only the dense, thick trees, still and waiting in the brightening light.

"Morning, Andy," she said, trying to keep her voice steady. "What evidence do we have so far?"

"Morning, May," he greeted her, his voice sharp and worried behind his mask. "This victim has been identified as Alyssa Darlington, who lives in Sevenfields."

May nodded, visualizing the nearby small town immediately. It was an affluent area, less than fifteen minutes' drive from Fairshore.

"The cause of death is strangulation, as I'm sure you can see. On her neck, there are clear signs that someone reached around to strangle her," the coroner continued. "The attacker is most likely right-handed." May nodded, grateful for this important early evidence as he continued. "The witness who found the body is over there. He said he is her boyfriend."

He inclined his head toward the young man standing with Sheriff Jack and the paramedics.

A boyfriend? This situation was getting more confusing. Why had he not been with her as she headed into the woods? May wondered. Or had he? she then thought, with a chill.

"Do we have a timeframe?" she asked, glad that she sounded as calm and controlled as she'd hoped.

"We received the call twenty minutes ago, and reached the scene five minutes ago. The death must have occurred very recently prior to our call."

"That's helpful," May said.

"There's nothing we can do for her now but the post-mortem," he continued. "We'll prioritize that, of course. All the vital evidence will be gathered and recorded. I hope it tells us something."

May nodded. Given how recent this timeframe was, the testimony of every person still at this after-party would be critical and could add something important.

She felt glad she'd asked the officer at the parking lot to prevent anyone from leaving.

But first and foremost, she needed to find out more from the witness who had discovered the body. Why was he covered in blood? What had played out?

"I think we should speak to him first," she said to Owen in a low voice. He looked at her gravely, before nodding.

Feeling purposeful now that the shock of seeing the body had subsided, May turned away from the crime scene and headed over to where the paramedics were at work.

CHAPTER THREE

As May walked over to where the dark-haired and good-looking young man was being attended to by the paramedics, she saw that he was sitting up on a waterproof sheet, staring ahead, with a lost, bewildered expression on his face.

He was holding a Kleenex to his nose, and his face was streaked with tears.

Sheriff Jack walked quickly up to greet her and Owen.

"I haven't been able to speak to this young man yet as the paramedics have been treating him. But we need to interview him urgently. Will you two handle this, and I will go and help manage the scene at the parking lot?"

"Yes, Jack," May replied, and he strode off.

May walked up to the paramedics.

"Is the witness ready for us to speak to him?" she asked.

"I think so, ma'am," the young woman replied in a low voice to May. "He says he's Dylan McDowell, boyfriend of the victim. He was in a very emotional state when we arrived, and had also gotten sick a few times. He told us he had already had several alcoholic drinks so we were monitoring him for signs of alcohol poisoning. Anyway, we have controlled his vomiting, given him some water and electrolytes, and treated minor scrapes on his hands and knees, so I don't think he's in any danger now, and can speak to you."

May approached the young man.

His hair was tousled and his eyes were traumatized. Turning, he looked at them unhappily.

"I'm Deputy Moore," she said, introducing herself. "And this is Deputy Lovell. We are going to ask you some questions, alright?"

"Alright," he said softly.

"You called this crime in? You found the body?"

"That's correct," Dylan said.

"What happened?"

May knelt down on the blanket herself, so she could be at eye level with him.

"I - I - it's so confusing." He was still sobbing softly. "We were in the woods, together, you know - making out? And Alyssa said she wanted a blanket, that she wasn't comfortable."

"Go on," May said.

"I remembered I had this camping sheet in my car. So I told her I would go get it. I - I didn't think I would be long. I went back to the parking lot to get it. I got it out of my car and I came back. And when I came back, I found her - I found her dead. That's it."

He shrugged miserably.

May frowned at him.

There seemed to be a multitude of holes in this sketchy story. The timeframe in particular seemed problematic. She was convinced that this was not the full truth and might not even be the partial truth.

Glancing at Owen, she saw his gaze was fixated on the blood on Dylan's shirt. He was clearly wondering how this witness had managed to get liberally streaked with blood on a simple trip to the car and back.

May decided it was no longer appropriate to question him here. This needed to be done more formally.

"Deputy Lovell and I are going to escort you to the car," she told him. "We're going to take you into the police department and you can give us a full statement there."

May stood up and helped the young man to his feet. He stumbled. He was clearly very drunk and she guessed his pallor was not just from shock.

She reached out her arm to steady him.

"Do you think you are able to walk?"

"I don't know," he whispered. "I don't feel very good."

"We'll get you to the car," she promised, and Owen took the young man's other arm and picked up the camping sheet.

As they escorted him out of the woods, May heard a shriek coming from the parking lot. Sheriff Jack was hurrying over to a couple who had just arrived.

"My son! What is going on? He called us to say there's been a crime! Where is he?" the blonde woman demanded. Then she uttered another appalled cry. "He's with the police!" she shouted, pointing in May's direction. She rushed over, again ignoring Jack's warning shout.

"Dylan! What happened?" she asked in a shaking voice. "Who hurt you?"

Dylan didn't answer. He hung his head, looking mortified.

"Was he attacked? What's all the blood on his shirt from?" Dylan's father asked, sounding shocked. He glared at May as if suspecting one of the police might have done something to his son.

"We don't yet know what happened. That's what we need to find out," May said. "Your son has received medical treatment for vomiting. He does not appear to have been attacked."

May glanced at Owen and gestured for him to open the back door of the police car for the witness.

"But where are you taking him? He needs to come home!" Mrs. McDowell insisted.

"We have to take him in to give us a statement," May explained. "We won't keep him long. But he's a witness to a murder, so we do need to ask him some questions."

The slim woman stared at her mutinously.

"Well, I demand that we be allowed to sit in on this. We need to hear what our son has to say. He's only seventeen. He's injured and he is ill and he should be going straight to the medical center."

Now, May looked at Sheriff Jack for guidance, knowing her boss would make the right call.

He nodded.

"Yes, Mr. and Mrs. McDowell," Jack said, sounding resigned, as if he didn't want to make this decision but yet, he felt it was best. "You can be in attendance. If you could please follow the police through to the Fairfield Police Department, the deputies will meet you there and you can sit in."

He nodded at them, his expression sympathetic.

May knew their presence would mean interference. Immediately, she could see they were those kind of people, with their behavior made worse by the fact they were upset and distraught. But all the same, it was the most sensible decision. Their son was underage and they had every right to sit in on the interview. In a small town, May knew, the police had to be considerate of locals and families. But undoubtedly it would make their job harder.

As Owen helped Dylan into the back of May's cruiser, she walked a few steps away from the group with Sheriff Jack.

"I've been speaking to the remaining party goers," he told her quietly. "Accounts are confused. There was definitely excessive drinking taking place. People were drunk. They're still drunk. And can't recall accurately."

May nodded. This confirmed her fears that it would be hard to get any coherent version of events.

Jack continued. "So far, nobody has heard or seen anything, but we have taken everyone's contact details before allowing them to leave. One thing I have ascertained, though, is that Dylan McDowell is not Alyssa's boyfriend. A number of the witnesses were very clear on that and volunteered the information without being asked. So we already seem to have an inconsistency in his version," he warned.

"Thanks for telling me," May said in a low voice. "I will make sure we ask him about that, and question him in a lot of detail." She knew she would have to do all she could to get to the truth.

"Good luck," Jack said. "I'll let you get on with that. I need to wrap up my interviews of the other students, and I've then got to speak to the parents of the victim, who are on their way." He sighed heavily and May knew the thought of this difficult task was already weighing on him.

Turning away, he headed over to the pavilion.

May turned back to the car, feeling overwhelmed by the complexity of this case.

They had a violent, senseless murder that was all the more painful for May to handle because the victim was so close in age to her sister, at the time of her disappearance.

They had hordes of drunk witnesses who would provide unreliable accounts.

The witness who had found the body was lying. He was covered in blood for reasons they hadn't yet found out. And his overwrought parents were clearly going to interfere in any way they could.

As she glanced back at the pavilion, she noticed that the red rose bush seemed to have fewer blooms than the pink and white ones.

Had the killer picked one of these roses to offer to the victim, or else deliberately plucked a rose, knowing that he was going to kill her and intending to scatter the petals over her body? she wondered suddenly. That was a creepy thought as it added another layer of complexity to the scenario.

May had the sinking feeling that this wasn't going to be a slam-dunk investigation. They had only just started, yet already she feared that this was going to be a long, difficult, painful case.

She hoped she would have what it took to cut through the lies, fend off the parents' interference, and fight her way to the truth. This interview would be a critically important first step.

CHAPTER FOUR

With Dylan and his parents sitting in the small interview room at the Fairfield police department, May thought the room felt cramped and airless. She wished they could open a window, but the only window was the small square of mirrored glass leading to the observation room where she knew Owen was monitoring the interview.

She did her best by turning on the aircon as cold as it would go.

Dylan looked miserable. His head was bowed. His breath reeked of alcohol.

Mrs. McDowell looked irate, protective, and fierce.

The air in the room felt charged with hostility, like a storm was approaching.

May had to admit that the couple appeared to have genuine concern for their son. However, she was not going to let that sway her from her duty.

"I have to ask you some questions," she said, looking at Dylan. He had his arms wrapped around himself, as if he was cold. He didn't reply and May knew the tone had been set. This was going to be a demanding session. But she had to get to the truth.

May was trying to decide what angle would work best to begin the questioning. She had the distinct feeling that things were not the way Dylan McDowell had told the story.

At that moment, Mrs. McDowell interrupted things.

"I know your mother," she said.

May's eyebrows shot up. This was not what she'd expected.

"You do?"

"We go to the same church. She's not always at the Sunday services." Mrs. McDowell looked at May through narrowed eyes, as if this was a definite character flaw that somehow counted against May, too. "But we've spoken quite regularly and we both helped with the last bake sale."

"Um, that's great," May began.

Clearly, Mrs. McDowell was hoping to use the connection somehow, probably to help get her son out of the interview room quicker.

"We're a good family. My son has a good heart. We've raised him well," she added. Her gaze pierced May like a skewer.

"Absolutely," May said.

She leaned forward, focusing once again on the unhappy looking witness. "Dylan, the quicker you tell us your story, the sooner we can all go home," she said as kindly as she could.

Dylan's head jerked up at the mention of his name and his gaze was shocked.

"I'm sorry," he mumbled, looking down again. "I'll try to answer."

"Were you and Alyssa dating?" May asked, wanting to get to the core of this inconsistency as soon as she could.

"Uh, look, not really. We were friends. Good friends."

"You said she was your girlfriend?"

May needed to dig deeper into this issue because a misunderstanding, a rejection, could potentially have exploded into violence. It was clear that Mr. McDowell had the same thought because he interrupted angrily.

"Does this seriously matter? I mean, girlfriend can mean someone who's a girl, and a friend. Why on earth are you arguing these semantics?"

"Yeah, I dunno, Dad," Dylan mumbled.

"It's important to get everything straight," May explained, making sure to sound non-judgmental.

"She was a friend, but we were, like, moving to being closer. I knew her really well. Ask anyone, we spent a lot of time together. And I said girlfriend because I didn't want anyone to think I was the type of guy who'd casually fool around with a girl."

Mrs. McDowell nodded approvingly. "Our boy has morals."

May accepted this explanation. But it didn't rule out that he could have been the killer, and it raised the question of whether he was the type of guy who would tell a bigger lie.

"W-will this take much longer?" Dylan asked, his voice sounding small and childlike.

"You have to understand, this is a serious matter, and we have to get everything straight. So I do have a few more questions," May said. "Next, I need you to tell me about your movements around the time of the crime. You went back to the car to get a blanket. How long did that take?"

"I told you already," he said mutinously. He was starting to seem combative, and May knew that his parents were only making things worse by being so protective of him, and being so antagonistic toward her.

May had a suspicion that Dylan McDowell was replying in this aggressive way because he was lying.

But how far?

Was he covering up a crime of passion in which he had lost control, or was he lying about something more minor?

May decided she was going to look at the minor details first.

"Where did you go when you returned back to the parking lot? Did you go straight to your car?"

Now he looked down, staring furiously at the desk.

May guessed there was something about the timeline of his actions that was an issue here.

"Did you speak to anyone?"

"Yes. I spoke to my friend George for a couple of minutes. We - we did a dare. Downing shots."

May understood now. Dylan was torn up that he hadn't gone directly back to Alyssa. And she could not argue the fact that if he wasn't the killer and he had gone straight back, then she might not have been murdered. His presence there could have kept the killer away.

However, Dylan was clever enough to realize that and there was no reason at all to labor this point. The guilt was probably eating away at him already. Nobody could possibly have known this would happen, and Alyssa had not necessarily been left in dangerous circumstances.

And if Alyssa had been targeted personally and the murderer had wanted to kill her specifically, then he would have made a plan to try again.

"So you then got the blanket and returned to the woods?"

"Yeah."

Now she saw relief in his eyes. Relief that he wasn't being judged for having spent time with his friend.

"Did you hear or see anything on your way back?" she asked.

He narrowed his eyes and she could tell he was thinking, really thinking, about this.

"I think I heard a scream, but at the time I thought it was from the party behind me. I didn't realize she was screaming," he said. "But now, I'm thinking it might have been her."

"You didn't mention that earlier."

"Well, I wasn't sure."

"Did you see anything?"

"No."

"Was she in a different place when you got back?"

He nodded. "Yeah, yeah, she was. She must have run - run from the guy. I arrived back and she was nowhere to be seen. I thought maybe I'd remembered wrong, and we'd actually gone further, so I walked ahead looking for her, with my phone flashlight on, and then I saw her ahead."

He buried his face in his hands.

His mother rubbed his back, looking daggers at May, which she felt was a little unfair because someone had to ask these questions. It wasn't May's fault that it was her.

"How did you come to be covered in blood?" she asked bluntly. Might as well move straight to the main reason why he was here, she thought.

"W-What?" Dylan stammered.

"Blood."

"Oh, yes. You see, when I got there, and I saw her, I thought - I thought maybe I could help her. Resuscitate her. I thought I could give her mouth to mouth and help her. I tried. I really tried."

He sounded agonized. There were tears in his eyes.

May thought this was genuine. She didn't detect a false note in what he said or what he had done. The strangulation had been from behind, and had clearly caused a bloody nose. Dylan had, in fact, tried to save her.

And George could hopefully confirm that they'd had a shots dare before he'd gone back to her.

One last question occurred to May.

"Are you right or left-handed?" she asked.

His mother replied for him. "He's left-handed, just like I am," she said proudly.

Again, that confirmed to May that he had not been the strangler, who the pathologist had said was right-handed, based on the injuries to Alyssa's neck.

"Thank you for telling me this," she said. "You've done a very good job in recalling it and staying calm. It's hard being questioned regarding a murder. It's tough on everyone and I am sorry that it has to be this way."

Finally, both parents looked satisfied by her praise of their son.

"You mentioned that you and Alyssa were close," May continued. "Did she tell you about any recent problems in her life? Any issues she had with anyone at the school, or who might have known about this post-prom party? Any conflict?"

She waited.

She could see Dylan felt very reluctant about this. And May thought, strongly, that he knew of someone but he didn't want to say.

"Not really," he mumbled.

This time, though, having his parents there worked in May's favor. She could see both the McDowells were very aware that any new suspect would take the focus off their son.

"You need to try and remember, honey," Mrs. McDowell insisted.

"Don't be scared, son. People must face the consequences," his father encouraged.

But Dylan had clearly spilled as much as he was prepared to.

"I don't really know any more," he insisted.

May decided to leave it there. She sensed that if she questioned any further, she'd only hit a blank wall. He'd told her enough for her to take this forward, and she was sure that she could find out more about this situation, and the conflict, from other people.

In particular, Alyssa's parents. May really didn't want to speak to them so soon after this tragedy. She knew already it was going to be a heartbreaking interview.

But she was sure Alyssa's parents would know more about their daughter's life, and be able to shed light on what Dylan had hinted at.

Hopefully, now that Sheriff Jack had broken the news, May could speak to them and try to find out more.

CHAPTER FIVE

Interviewing the parents of a murder victim had to be the most soul-destroying part of a murder investigation, and it always resonated deeply with May because of her own past. She and Owen drove to Alyssa's home, in Sevenfields, in silence.

It was a glorious morning and this small town, in a valley among green hills, had always impressed May with its serene charm. Beside her, Owen's heavy sigh told her that he, too, was feeling terrible about having to drive into this picturesque village, with its historic church, its park, its well kept homes – to talk to bereaved parents about their daughter.

Sheriff Jack had called May earlier to say the parents were headed home and were prepared to speak to her, so at least she knew they'd had a short time to take in the devastating news and had readied themselves to talk.

"Here we are." This was their home, number three Terrace Drive. A double-story house with a bright, tiled roof and a garden exploding with colorful blooms in well-tended flower beds.

May climbed out of the car and trod up the garden path, feeling her heart heavy in her chest.

She knocked on the door, exchanging a glance with Owen that spoke volumes.

The door was opened by a woman in her mid-forties, tall and beautiful, with a tear-stained face.

"Deputy Moore and Deputy Lovell," May introduced herself and Owen in a gentle voice. "Mrs. Darlington?"

"Yes," the woman said hoarsely. "The sheriff said you'd be here. I don't really feel prepared to talk, but I need to find out who did this. I need to!"

May saw her eyes flash. This woman might be heartbroken, but May could see she had a core of steel.

"Thank you," she said softly.

"My husband is with our other children," Mrs. Darlington continued. "We have three younger children. Alyssa was our oldest. So I'll talk to you alone," she said.

Taking a deep, shaky breath, Mrs. Darlington led the way into the home, which May was impressed to see was immaculately tidy.

She sat down on a white leather couch in the lounge and motioned for May and Owen to sit.

"Mrs. Darlington, we need to know a few more details about Alyssa's personal life. We don't yet know why she was targeted or who the killer is, so we're hoping to get a better picture of this, if you're able to tell us?" May said.

"Sure. Sure. What do you want to know? She is – was – a high achiever. She did well academically. Top grades in math and science. She liked sports. And she was a beauty. I guess, well I always thought of her as my golden girl. You know, she missed being prom queen by a couple of points?"

That intrigued May. Had this beautiful young woman gotten herself into a complicated situation where jealousy might have been a motive?

"Was Alyssa dating anyone?"

Mrs. Darlington shook her head. "No. She wasn't dating at the time of her death."

"And before that?" Owen asked. He was clearly also focused on getting a picture of any emotions that might have been in play. Something could have been destructive enough to trigger murder. If it had, they needed to know more.

Mrs. Darlington frowned. "She dated one of the boys in her class, Miles, for a couple of months earlier this year, but she broke up with him a few weeks ago."

That timeframe might be important, May thought.

"What did you think of him?" she asked.

She had to wait a minute while Mrs. Darlington buried her face in her hands again, overcome by another wave of grief. Owen jumped up and passed her a handful of Kleenex from the box that had clearly been placed on the otherwise empty coffee table for this reason.

May watched, feeling deeply sympathetic. She thought Mrs. Darlington was holding things together incredibly well. She was being as helpful as she could. May hoped that in some way she was finding it comforting to talk about this.

"I never liked Miles," she said eventually. "I wasn't happy with Alyssa going out with him. He was a bit of a wild one. He was a star football player with an ego. He liked to drink. He liked to party. And I didn't like him personally."

"Why's that?" May said.

"He was a real bully. He was controlling. He was one of those boys you don't want your daughter to date, but of course they end up getting drawn to because at that age, they can't make the differentiation between controlling and strong."

May nodded sympathetically, but at the same time she was very interested in the direction this was going.

"Did he break up with her, or she with him?" May asked.

"Well, they broke up twice," Mrs. Darlington said. "The first time, she said she was tired of being pushed around and she promised that she wasn't going back to him, but of course she did. Then a few weeks later, he dumped her. And to make it worse, he started dating one of her friends, Candace Holliday."

"Go on," May said.

"Candace actually ended up being prom queen. But that's beside the point. The point was that Alyssa felt mad about the whole situation. She thought she'd been treated unfairly. She thought he was a user, and that others needed warning about that."

May thought this was interesting and important.

"Did she ever talk about that to you? Was she planning to do anything or tell anyone?"

"She just said he was a jerk and that he should get what was coming to him. I warned her that revenge can be a double-edged sword, and she then said that was true and she agreed, because if he knew she'd caused trouble, he would make sure there was payback."

May caught Owen's astonished glance at her, out of the corner of her eye. This was very significant. Had there been payback?

"Did she say anything else?" May asked.

"We didn't speak about it again. She didn't always tell me what was going on in her life, although we were fairly close. I think she would have left it. But now, I am wondering."

"Did she suspect he might be violent? Did she ever mention to you that he had been violent or abusive, or threatening, to her?"

"She mentioned something one time about his past. We were having a mother-daughter argument at the time because she'd gotten back home way after her curfew. And I can't remember exactly what she said, but it was something along the lines of how I should just back off because she was doing just fine, she was staying out of trouble, she hadn't messed up in life the way Miles had."

May thought, from what Mrs. Darlington was saying, that there might be more to this.

"Was there anything else troubling Alyssa in the past couple of weeks? Anything that she told you, or didn't tell you, or that you picked up?"

Mrs. Darlington thought carefully about that.

"Nothing comes to mind at all," she said.

"Thank you," May replied. "I really appreciate that you've been able to tell us so much."

She never knew what to say at the end of an interview like this. Even the most heartfelt words of sympathy were surely going to seem empty compared to the extent of the bereavement this mother was coping with. But even so, she had to try.

"We're all so torn up about this. I can't imagine what you're enduring. Please understand we are going to work as hard as we can to solve this crime and find out what happened."

"I appreciate that," Alyssa's mother said, now in tears all over again thanks to May's kind words.

They got up and walked out, quietly and respectfully. May blinked hard when she was outside in the bright sun again. This emotional interview had been important. It had presented them with a potential killer, who might have had a motive for revenge, and might also have past issues that were relevant.

Miles Taylor had reason to resent Alyssa. There had been complicated issues between them, probably more so than she knew, especially if Alyssa had made good on her threats of payback.

On prom night, seeing his new girlfriend crowned as prom queen, there was a definite chance that Alyssa might have done what she promised, and disaster could have followed.

Miles Taylor was a strong suspect and she and Owen needed to speak to him as soon as they could.

CHAPTER SIX

Sadie Croft walked along the track by the lake, pulling her thick, auburn hair over her face, wanting to hide from the world.

She felt hungover, tired, and shocked after the murder at the post-prom party which she'd heard about as she had left.

She hadn't known Alyssa well, and could not imagine what could have happened to cause this, or how it had felt for her. She felt sad for her, and terribly guilty, too.

What if someone had gotten high on her stash and that was why they'd done what they did to that girl? Had Sadie's actions at the party put Alyssa into an early grave?

She felt cold suddenly, and goose bumps prickled on her skin.

Sadie knew that for a few years now, she'd been the unofficial go-to for illegal drugs, including some prescription drugs, which she sold to selected contacts and friends at school.

But she feared now that she couldn't afford to do that anymore. The police would be watching everyone closely. The sheriff had questioned her before she'd left and she'd been terrified that he would search her and find the contraband in her inside jacket pocket.

She'd been equally terrified that someone she'd sold to would have squealed on her and the police would take her in. Luckily she'd been one of the first to leave.

No, if she wanted to stay out of jail, things had to change. She was going to have to give the game up. And she was going to have to find some other way to earn some money.

Sadie took the pills out of her pocket and stared down at them.

She wasn't a bad person, but she knew she had done something seriously wrong, and had been lucky to get away with it.

Still, she couldn't believe that might have been the reason for what had happened. She hadn't seen anything when she'd been at the party. But it had gotten very out of control. She knew she hadn't been aware of everything happening that night, and she was feeling scared.

One thing was for sure, she couldn't go home. Not until she got this taken care of. She didn't want to go back to the house. What was there for her, anyway? Her mom would be drinking, as she often did during the day. She worked nights at a bar near the industrial area of Chestnut Hill.

Her dad had moved out – as he did periodically – and she didn't know where he was at the moment.

She should throw the remaining tablets away. Just toss them into the lake.

But as she took out the package and looked at them, her mind started adding up what they were worth. They were worth almost a hundred dollars to those who would buy them.

That was a hundred dollars that Sadie needed. She stared at the water as she walked.

The lake rippled gently, almost hypnotically. But Sadie didn't like it. She didn't like the town, and how small it was here. How everyone was in everyone else's business all the time.

Sadie wanted to get away from this place. She wanted to get away from her friends and connections, and the whole scene. Making a fresh start had never appealed more.

She had a strong feeling that they were all going to get in trouble for what had happened.

Sighing, Sadie turned away from the lake and headed along the trail leading to the woods. There was a clearing a couple hundred yards ahead where she could sit, smoke some weed. It was miles from anywhere and she knew nobody would notice her there.

She'd been here before, too often. For years, she'd come here whenever she needed a way to escape.

To hide.

People seldom came to this part of the trail.

She had a little weed in her pocket, for when she reached the clearing. For now, Sadie groped in her pocket and found her cigarettes, though there weren't many left. She'd need to get more soon.

As she headed into the woods, Sadie heard footsteps behind her.

Surprised, she glanced around.

Tall trees lined the narrow, winding trail. She couldn't see anyone there.

But for some reason, hearing those steps made her feel extremely jumpy. It was only natural to feel spooked, she told herself, looking back again. After all, one of her classmates had been murdered this morning.

It was probably because she felt vulnerable alone in the woods. This hadn't worked out the way she'd planned. She'd come out here so that she wouldn't have to think about the murder at all. Now here she was, feeling like a girl in the movies, being chased down by some crazy madman. She needed to get a grip on herself.

Sadie walked toward the clearing, deeper and deeper into the woods.

She tried to comfort herself by thinking about her fresh start. It was possible, but she might need to sell more of her stash first. With as little as a few hundred dollars, she could get away. And if she worked hard, she could earn it fast, and break free from everything that was chaining her here.

But then, she heard the footsteps again, interrupting her thoughts. They were keeping pace with her. Someone was following.

She looked around again but could see only trees. Whoever it was, they were still some distance behind.

Sadie slowed right down, feeling unsettled, listening hard. Hopefully, whoever it was would then pass her on the trail.

But now, walking slower, she couldn't hear the footsteps at all.

She took the last drag of her cigarette and threw it on the forest floor.

She turned around quickly.

"Hello?" she called.

Nobody was there.

Maybe she had heard something – or maybe she was just paranoid. She was feeling a little squirrely. And she was angry with herself to have chosen a trail that followed such a twisting path. She couldn't see more than a few yards behind her at any time because the trees were in the way. That hadn't been a wise choice.

She hurried on a little faster, trying to get ahead of the footsteps.

But now, they had started up again and they were keeping pace with her.

She didn't like this. Not at all.

Turning again, straining her eyes, she peered back into the murk of trees. Her heart was thumping.

"Is anyone there?" she called into the dimness.

There was no reply. The woods felt cool and hushed.

Something was wrong here. As she stood in the darkened woods, she began to get a hollow feeling in the pit of her stomach.

Now, she could hear the distinctive sound of feet crunching through the undergrowth. Someone was treading toward her. Fast.

And Sadie finally saw the figure.

She stared, in utter surprise. She recognized this walker.

"It's you?" she said. Her voice was shaky. She still felt scared, though not as scared as she had been. Not now that she saw who it was.

But then her mind started screaming at her that it was surely one huge coincidence to meet this person out here, in the middle of nowhere, at such a time. And furthermore, he hadn't said a word to her. Highly unusual.

But he was looking at her with a predatory gleam in his eyes that she'd never seen before, and which petrified her. And he was hurrying toward her. Purposeful. Intent. Silent.

That's when Sadie began to run.

She knew, instinctively, that nothing about this encounter was normal and that if he got any closer, she'd be in terrible danger.

"Help me!" she screamed, as she heard running footsteps, hard and fast, pursuing her.

But she knew nobody could hear her.

She turned her head, already knowing that it was a mistake, that she should use all her energy for speed.

He was close behind, gasping, grinning as he ran. His outstretched hands were reaching for her. Terrified, Sadie began to beg.

"No! Please, no!" she cried. But he was deaf to her pleas.

His arms knocked her roughly forward. Losing her balance, she sprawled on the ground.

He was on her now and his hands were at her throat. They wrapped tighter. She couldn't breathe and she started clawing at his wrists. She wanted to fight him, to get another chance and to do things a better way. Choose a safer route.

But he was too strong. The world was going dark around her.

And then there was blackness.

CHAPTER SEVEN

"What did you make of what Mrs. Darlington said about Miles Taylor?" May asked Owen, as they climbed into the car, wondering if he was thinking along the same lines as her.

"It sounds like that situation could have contributed to what happened last night. And he sounds like the kind of guy we should be speaking to. Violent tendencies."

"Yes. That definitely seemed to be an issue. In fact, I was wondering if we should check his history. It definitely seems that he might have a past. If he was very abusive, he might have gotten into trouble with the law."

"Would the school tell us if he had?" Owen asked.

May made a face. "There might be confidentiality issues. And, at seven a.m. on a Sunday, we might lose time finding that out. How about we go and look it up? We're close to the Sevenfields police department. We could stop in there and ask if we can access the database."

"Good idea," Owen said.

The police department was just a few streets ahead, and May personally thought it was the prettiest one in the whole of Tamarack County. It was a tiny, cottage-like building, set across the road from a garden center and coffee shop. Being across the road from a garden center, grateful residents had donated plants, as well as time, to creating the most beautiful mini-garden, with pot plants, small hedges, and flower beds surrounding the entrance.

May parked outside, walked in, and greeted the mustached sergeant at the desk, who was drinking coffee.

"Morning, Anthony."

"Morning, May and Owen. Are you here about this prom party murder? We've had quite a few people calling in and asking about it. People are already feeling unsafe."

May nodded. "We have just interviewed her mother."

Anthony made a face. "That must have been difficult."

"It was. We do have a lead, and want to do some research before we go further. Can we go into your back office and have a seat for a minute to access the database?"

"Sure. The deputy's not here, so the office is free. Please, go through and use the spare desk on the right. I hope it helps you."

Quickly, May and Owen walked down the short passage, and into the sunny back office. They sat down at the desk and wasted no time logging in to access the records they needed.

It seemed like eons, but was probably just a few seconds, before the right database opened and they could search for the name they needed.

"Well, that's interesting. Miles Taylor does have a record," Owen said.

May narrowed her eyes. "But it's from last year. And he was a juvenile at that stage so it's sealed."

"Any chance we can get a warrant and have the records unsealed?" Owen asked.

"Doubtful."

"Maybe we don't really need to read it," Owen suggested. "I mean, any crime is relevant, right? It shows he was a lawbreaker."

"Well, some crimes might be more relevant to this case than others. For example, shoplifting would be less relevant. Assault would be more relevant," May argued. There was an important distinction between crimes, and knowing what he'd done would help them, but she didn't see any way of finding out more.

Unless she could ask her sister.

The thought occurred to her, unwelcome and uncomfortable. The FBI could access some of the juvenile records. Kerry might be able to tell her more.

But was it right to do that?

May thought about that for a while.

She didn't have the ability to access sealed records. That was not within her jurisdiction as a county deputy. Was she going to break the rules and put herself in debt to her sister - especially with the upcoming wedding, and all the 'small favors' and the unspoken threat of being asked to be maid of honor?

May decided it would be unwise. This was not the time to get into debt with Kerry. Especially when there was another way to get the information. After all, this was a small town.

She picked up the phone and called Sheriff Jack, hoping that the police network in this community might end up being as effective as the FBI.

Jack picked up, sounding tired.

"Hello, May. What a situation this is," he said grimly. "Too many drunk teens. Too many confused versions. How did your questioning go?"

"We've cleared Dylan," May said. "And we've just interviewed Alyssa's mother, who has given us another lead. It's her ex-boyfriend, a football player called Miles Taylor. Apparently there was bad blood between them."

"That so?" Jack asked in concern.

"Miles has a record," May then explained. "We're here at the Sevenfields police department to look it up. We've accessed it, but it's sealed, because he was a minor at the time. He lives in Hazelwood, at number two Lantern Lane. Do you remember that crime at all? Was it recent?"

As the county sheriff, she was sure Jack would have been involved, or else know who to call.

"Hazelwood falls under the Smoky Pines police department," Jack said thoughtfully. "I know the deputy in charge well. And the name Miles Taylor is familiar to me. I think this crime was recent. I'll give the deputy a call straight away, and let you know."

"We'll get on our way to Miles's residence now," May said.

Feeling thankful that she'd thought of the quickest and most sensible route to get the information she needed, she stood up and hurried out of the police department, calling a quick thank you to Anthony on the way out.

Hazelwood was one of the wealthiest districts in Tamarack County, May knew. It was about ten minutes from here, in a beautiful location overlooking the lake.

"I wonder what Miles's parents do for a living," she said aloud as they climbed into the cruiser. After the recent interference Dylan's parents had given her, she felt wary that more of the same might happen.

"If it's the Taylors I know of, they own a chain of grocery stores. Not just in Tamarack County, but other areas of Minnesota too," Owen said.

May pulled off. It was a quiet Sunday morning, with little traffic on the road. Their town was peaceful, apart from the ripples and waves she knew were upsetting the community caused by this awful murder.

"Are those the Food Emporium stores?" she asked.

"Yes. Those are the ones," Owen confirmed.

May nodded. Owning so many stores, the Taylors would definitely be well off. They might well be looking to protect their son and could easily afford lawyers.

May felt nervous heading into this confrontation.

They had no choice. They had to speak to Miles. It was an important lead. May would just have to figure out the best way to handle him, when they got face to face.

As they drove, Owen began chatting to her, and May was grateful to him for taking her mind off the worrying interview ahead.

"There's a nice little art gallery in Hazelwood," he said. "It's called Art on the Lake. It's on the main street. I've been meaning to go in there. It's a family-run business and their art is really good. They have a lot of local artists whose work is on display. Do you know about it?"

"If it's the one on the corner, I've seen it," May said. "I love art. And I need to buy some paintings for my cottage. I have always thought how pretty the gallery looks, but I've always had work to do, so I've never been inside," she admitted.

"Shame we don't have time to stop in now," Owen said. "But I'll tell you what. If you're in the area and want to go, I'll go with you some time."

She glanced at him. "We might have time to visit it when this case is closed," she said.

"There's a great little restaurant next door," Owen said, clearly warming to his plans. "Maybe one day, when the case is solved, perhaps on a weekend, we could go look at the art and then head next door for a meal?"

The tall deputy was staring at her with an expectant look on his face, May realized, as she turned off the main road, following the signs for Hazelwood. It was almost as if he seemed slightly nervous about her answer.

She was too nervous about the upcoming confrontation with the Taylors to really take in what he was saying.

"That sounds like a great plan," she agreed hesitantly.

She thought that Owen wanted to say something else, but at that moment, May's phone rang. It was Sheriff Jack.

"Did you get any information?" she asked anxiously.

"I did," he confirmed. "I spoke to the arresting officer, who confirmed that Miles Taylor was arrested, and fined, for physically assaulting one of the girls in his class. I believe he punched her in the jaw, among other things. It happened last year, when he was seventeen."

May felt shock surge inside her.

Arrested for assaulting a woman! That was a serious and relevant offense. Their suspect had a recent track record of violence, as well as a clear grudge against Alyssa.

May thought they were on to something important here.

As she turned into Lantern Lane, she wondered if they were about to reach the home of Alyssa's killer.

"I think this is it. Their house should be the first one on the right." Her mouth felt dry.

"Yes," Owen said, checking the map.

They pulled into the Taylors' driveway, a long, sweeping, oak-lined approach. The house itself was impressive, a large mansion with massive sheet windows, a portico, pillars and a triple garage. May parked next to the garage doors, on the neat, red brick paving.

Climbing out, she swallowed down her nerves.

"I hope this goes smoothly," she said.

"I hope so, too," Owen agreed.

But then, May frowned, turning to the house in surprise.

The front door was open. She could hear raised voices coming from inside. Men were shouting. There seemed to be a massive fight taking place.

She glanced at Owen in consternation. Had they interrupted a crime? Was there a robbery in progress? Hesitantly, May reached for her gun, wondering if she would need it.

And the next moment, there was a crash of glass.

Two figures burst out of a sheet window and landed on the manicured grass, yelling and wrestling furiously.

CHAPTER EIGHT

May knew there was no time to think, no time to hesitate, only time to rush in and break up this violent struggle. It was not a job for guns, but rather for immediate physical intervention to manage this aggressive fight. Together, she and Owen raced forward. May's shoes sank into the lush, soft grass as she rushed to the wrestling pair.

Owen grabbed the shoulders of the nearest man and dragged him out of the way as he was yelling and punching.

Hoping that she'd be strong enough to do her part, May lunged for the arm of the other man and held onto it fiercely as the man struggled and tried to wrench himself away.

He was snarling and swearing in a splutter of rage.

But May kept her grip. She knew she had to get this fight controlled fast. The men were so angry, so enraged, she was not sure what each one might be capable of.

She wasn't even sure yet who was the intruder.

"Get off me!" the tall, heavyset man roared as she yanked him backward.

"Police! Break it up, now!" May yelled as firmly as she could. "This fight has to stop!"

The man turned his head, his face contorted with rage. He was younger than she'd expected, with well-cut brown hair and angry blue eyes and a couple of small lacerations on his forehead and hands from the glass.

His face was familiar. In fact, she recognized him from the photos she'd just been perusing to become more familiar with the suspect.

This angry young man was Miles Taylor himself!

Miles Taylor was a big, muscular young man who, in his rage, reminded May of a bull. And here he was, struggling on his own lawn, having just burst clean through a window.

May gasped in shock.

What was going on here?

"Calm down, please, sir," she repeated firmly.

Now that Miles saw his opponent was also being held, he was not struggling as violently. Quickly, May turned to Owen. The other man was still clearly furious and had plenty to say.

"Let me at him! I have to teach my stepson a hard lesson," the older man raged.

Again, May felt sideswiped by shock.

This was Miles's stepdad? He'd been fighting so fiercely with his stepdad that they'd burst right through a window? This was totally unacceptable on both their parts, but particularly the stepdad who must have started this fight. What kind of a role model had Miles grown up with, if this was the behavior he'd been taught?

"You have no right to bully me!" Miles snarled back, clearly unrepentant.

"You stole my car!" the stepdad raged, scrambling to his feet as Owen hung on with all his might. He was also a big, strong guy, May noted, with thick, sandy-blonde hair and a glower on his fleshy face.

"I did not! Stop accusing me like that in front of the police!" Miles protested, but now May heard a note of panic in his tone.

"Let go of me! I have to teach this guy a lesson!" the stepdad roared at Owen.

"Not as yet, sir, I'm afraid," Owen stated calmly.

"He stole my car last night. He took it out, without permission, and now it has a big scratch along the side. It's a Porsche Cayenne! Damaged, because this idiot boy was joyriding in it!"

"You're lying," Miles protested. "There was no way it was me. You just have a grudge against me!"

"A grudge? I have a grudge? You stole my car and crashed it. I opened the garage this morning, and there was the damaged car, to prove it!" His face was dark with rage.

For a moment, May wondered if the two men might start fighting again. She held on tightly to Miles's strong arm, ready to apply more force if necessary to keep him in line.

"I need to speak to you, Mr. Taylor," she said firmly.

"Not now! He's attacking me! He's going to kill me!" Miles yelled.

"No," the stepdad snarled. "You're going to jail, you little monster!"

"That's enough," May said, shocked by the menace in both men's voices. They were like two bulls butting heads, she thought.

She decided to take charge, before these two men ripped each other apart.

"You are coming with me," she told Miles firmly.

"Like hell I will," he shrieked. "You're not arresting me. I won't go to jail. I'm innocent! He started this."

"We didn't come here because you two were fighting. We came to speak to you about a different matter," May said, keeping her voice neutral yet firm. "I want to talk to you about Alyssa Darlington."

Instantly, Miles's expression hardened. His blue eyes narrowed to slits.

May didn't know how much he knew. If he was the killer, he was giving nothing away.

"What the hell? About her? No way, man, I don't know what's going on but I'm not the person you need," he snarled, trying to yank his arm away.

"Take him in. Lock him up. For the night, or better still, a few weeks," the stepfather snarled. "Now, if you can please let my arm go, officer, I need to call a panel beater." He glanced at the broken window. "And a glazier."

May turned Miles in the direction of the police cruiser, feeling relieved when Owen let go of the stepdad and grabbed his other arm. As May walked him to the vehicle, she noticed, through the open garage door, a silver Porsche Cayenne with a deep scratch all along one side.

She couldn't blame the stepfather for being mad, May decided, but that physical attack had been completely out of line. It was borderline dangerous behavior. She decided that when this was over, she'd come back and have a private chat with him about that. But now it was time to find out how far Miles's illegal activities had gone last night.

*

Twenty minutes later, Miles was installed in the Fairfield police department's interview room. With his elbows on the desk, he made the wooden chair seem small. He looked full of anger and, May thought, also rather hungover. He'd clearly been driving under the influence, which was another concern, although they couldn't prove it now.

Sitting opposite him next to Owen, May observed him for a minute, collecting her thoughts before speaking and deciding on the best way to open the conversation. She went for shock value in the end.

"Alyssa Darlington was murdered early this morning," May said, wanting to see his reaction.

He jolted in surprise.

"What? Are you joking? Are you saying this to try and trick me into something? I knew she was dead, but my friends told me it had been some kind of accident. That was what the rumors were!"

He surged to his feet so fast he knocked the chair over. Every bad feeling about this young man came flooding back to her.

"Sit down! Sit down immediately!" May ordered.

Miles glared at her but he sat, slowly.

"Alyssa was murdered," she repeated. "I'm sorry to have to tell you that."

"I don't believe it. She was at the post-prom party. She looked fine. What happened?"

"She was found dead in the early hours of this morning. It's true, Mr. Taylor. I'm sorry," May said.

"I still don't believe it. I don't accept this at all. I want proof of it. But if it's true, I had nothing to do with it." His face was rigid, his eyes unblinking.

"You dated her recently?" May asked.

"Look I wouldn't call it dating. We went out once or twice. She might have exaggerated things. Probably did."

Owen cleared his throat, turning his iPad toward their suspect.

"Her mother confirmed it with us just now. And look here. On your social media page here, just two months ago, it said 'In a Relationship With - Alyssa Darlington.' There are lots of comments from your friends saying, 'About time, wondered when you were going to publish this' and 'You make a lovely couple.'"

May felt extremely proud of Owen's quick thinking. Miles on the other hand, looked mortified.

"Yeah, okay, we broke up recently. It didn't work out. I admit it turned nasty. We both threatened each other with stuff. But then I started dating Candace, who ended up being the prom queen. And it all calmed down again. Why would I care about Alyssa when I was with the prom queen last night?"

"She might have cared. She might have wanted some kind of payback when she saw you together."

Miles shook his head. "Maybe she thought about that. But she didn't do anything."

He looked thoughtful. May wondered if he was thinking of his own reputation for violence.

"Were you with Candace last night? Do you have proof of where you were?"

Miles put his hand on his chin, thinking.

"We left the post-prom party at about one a.m. We went joyriding through town. Then we went to a nightclub in Chestnut Hill."

"Can you confirm that?" May asked sternly.

"Would that have been in your stepdad's car?" Owen asked curiously.

"Yeah. Yeah, it was."

"I took a photo of the car when we were there just now," Owen said. "Give me a moment, May. I'll check something." He got up and quickly walked out.

"You need proof?" Miles asked. May could see he was now getting a little scared. The implications were sinking in, after his initial denial. He was now applying himself to this interview and taking it seriously. "Um, I guess so. I mean, I paid cash to get in the club. I was with Candace the whole time. We took some selfies there. She sent them to me."

Now, May was sure he'd realized the potential seriousness of his predicament.

He reached for his phone and scrolled through, looking panicked. As he began showing her the nightclub shots, Owen walked back in.

"I've done a quick check. That number plate does appear on the traffic offense list for last night. You've got fines from several speeding cameras. At one-thirty a.m. on the way to Chestnut Hill, and at four-thirty a.m. on the way back to Hazelwood."

"I had no idea I was going that fast," Miles mumbled.

"If I were you, I'd explain to your stepdad, because if he finds out the hard way, you might end up having to call out the glazier again," Owen reprimanded him.

"I will. I will." Now Miles looked thoroughly subdued.

Immediately, May realized this cleared him, as he would not have been at the party during the window of time when Alyssa was murdered. She was now satisfied that he could not have killed Alyssa.

Unfortunately, that now left them with no new suspects, and she guessed they would need to go back to the drawing board and look at the witness reports they had so far.

But, at that moment, there was a knock on the interview room door.

May stood up quickly.

Sheriff Jack was at the door and instantly she saw from his face that something bad had happened.

He beckoned her outside.

"May, there has been another murder," he said in quiet, but hard, tones. "I don't believe this, but it's happened. One of the other students

40

who was at this party has just been found dead. I interviewed her early this morning, before she left. Without a doubt, we're dealing with a serial killer here."

CHAPTER NINE

May simply could not believe this bombshell, as she and Owen sped along the road, following Sheriff Jack's cruiser as he rushed to the crime scene.

Another murder. May felt utterly shocked that this had happened again. It changed the landscape of the entire investigation. The thoughts were whirling round and round in her mind. Who was doing this and why?

Was there a connection with the prom that the students had all attended? What was the motive?

"What's going on, May?" Owen said, sounding as confused as she felt.

"I wish I knew," May replied.

"Could it be someone who got mad at both these girls at the prom?" Owen suggested in mystified tones.

"We need to look for any connection. Any relationship we can find now will help us," May agreed.

Jack was heading out to a remote part of the lake shore, more than ten miles from the previous crime scene, May saw. He veered onto a dirt road and followed it a few hundred yards out to where the scenic lake and the woods converged.

Her heart plummeted as she saw the two police cars and the coroner's van parked by the side of the road, gleaming in the early afternoon sun. She pulled up beside them and climbed out.

A policeman was waiting at the trail head, looking anxious and alarmed.

"The scene is down this trail. Just follow it for a minute or two, and you'll get there. I'm staying here to redirect any walkers or hikers to an alternative route."

"Thank you," May said.

As fast as possible, she strode into the shadowy woods, desperately trying to figure out how, and why, another crime could have occurred here.

It would only be a matter of hours before the lakeside communities learned of this new murder, and the situation exploded in panic.

42

One murder was bad enough. But at a prom, with people drunk and high and out of control, there was the likelihood it had been a crime of passion and it was easier to explain without a general fear infecting the population.

Now, in the light of afternoon, a second killing meant the opposite. May knew people would feel unsafe. They needed to catch the killer before fingers were pointed at the police by terrified and furious citizens.

Here was the scene ahead. A policeman was standing beside a man with two dogs. The elderly man was sitting on a tree stump near the edge of the trail. The dogs were sitting in front of him, quiet and obedient.

"Afternoon, Deputy Moore," the policeman said. "The gentleman here, walking his dogs, called this crime in half an hour ago. We asked him to stay in case you have any questions."

She turned to look down the trail. The police crime scene tape was already in place, closing off the path. The coroner was already gowned up and examining the victim. May couldn't see her, beyond the knot of people.

And the elderly man wanted to talk. He was dressed in a pale blue shirt, holding the leashes of two friendly looking dogs that May guessed were Labrador crosses. Their tails thumped in greeting as May petted them.

"I found her on my daily walk," the man said. "I usually take a different route, but for some reason my dogs wanted to go this way so I changed things up and took this trail. I know there's usually no people out here at this time. It's the most terrible thing I've ever seen. Did I hear correctly that this is the second murder of young women?"

"That's correct," May said. "Did you see or hear anything unusual on your walk?"

He shook his head. "Not a thing. The woods were as quiet as always. I got a massive fright when I saw her there. At first I thought maybe she'd collapsed for some reason, but when I came closer I realized without a doubt she was dead."

"Then what did you do?" May asked.

"Well, I got my phone straight out of my pocket and called 911. And then I stayed here. I thought if the killer was still around, I had my dogs with me."

"That was very brave of you. Thank you," May said, even though she thought these dogs would be more likely to lick a criminal to death than provide any other type of protection.

But May could see the killer had come and gone. She suspected this body had been here a while, and if not for the dog walker, might only have been discovered much later.

"I'll take your name and details, sir." Owen moved forward with his notepad, taking over this short interview as May walked closer to where the coroner was at work.

She bit her lip as she looked down at the body.

This young woman was also beautiful, May saw sadly. She had pale, perfect skin and long, glowing copper hair. She was dressed in a T-shirt, jeans, and sneakers, so she must have changed out of her prom outfit and been on a walk.

It looked to May, from the marks she could see on the neck, like exactly the same method of attack. The women were being strangled from behind. The killer must have chased this woman in the same way, and then killed her in the same way.

Her eyes widened as she saw petals scattered around the body. These were not rose petals. Staring around, she guessed they had been ripped from the banks of wildflowers surrounding the path, although by now they were a little shriveled and wilted.

Why the petals? And why from behind, she wondered. Was there a reason for this whole ritual? If so, what could it be?

"Same MO," Andy Baker confirmed grimly. "And the scene is very clean. Unfortunately we don't even have a footprint, in all these leaves and mulch. You'll notice there are also flowers scattered at the scene?"

"Yes. What do you make of that?"

He shook his head. "It must mean something. To the killer, at least."

"What about the time of death?" May asked.

"I would say, between two and four hours ago, based on the preliminary body temperature and evidence," Andy explained. "That might vary by an hour outside of that, but not much more."

May checked the time. That meant this woman had been killed somewhere between breakfast and lunch time. That would have been after the police had arrived at the post-prom party.

In terms of timeframes, that cleared both Dylan and Miles. Dylan was in the care of his parents. Miles had mostly spent that time at the police station.

So, undoubtedly, another killer was at work and they had to widen the search.

"Do we have an ID for the victim?"

"Yes, we do," the coroner said. "She had her driver's license and student card in her pocket, along with a few illegal drugs. A bag of marijuana, and a few 'uppers' - party drugs, and one or two pharmaceutical drugs. I don't know if they were for personal use or whether she was sharing, or selling, them. Her name is Sadie Croft. She lives outside Chestnut Hill, a couple of miles from here."

"I interviewed her as she was leaving the party," Sheriff Jack said. "She told me that she hadn't had an invite, that she didn't see herself as part of the 'in' crowd, but she'd come along nevertheless."

"Maybe to make some money selling pills?" May suggested.

"Could be," Sheriff Jack replied. "We'll need to find out who she spoke to and what her movements were. I'm going to go and break the news to her mother now. We've already established that, as it's a serial, the murders are probably not related to the victims' personal lives, but I will rule that out all the same, and ask her, if she's able to answer."

"Thank you," May said, feeling relieved that the task of facing another bereaved parent would not fall to her again.

"If I find any other evidence, I'll let you know," Andy said, before turning back to his work, his eyes serious over his mask.

May thought that they had found as much as they would in this remote murder scene. She guessed there were no further clues to be had. The only way that they would find answers would be to go back and re-interview all of the students who had been at that post-prom party. They would need to ask again about who they saw there, if anyone unusual had been there, and if they had noticed either Sadie or Alyssa interacting with anyone suspicious at the party or in the days before. Then they would need to widen their parameters and ask all the teachers the same questions.

May had no illusions that it would be hard work and that it might well be unrewarding. By the time the students had processed the shock of the murder, by the time they'd sobered up and been around their parents - who might be mad at them, scared for them, or simply over-emotional - May knew they were not going to get many accurate accounts of what had played out that night.

She wondered if they should start with the teachers, who would at least have been more sober. She guessed it wasn't beyond the bounds of possibility that a teacher could have committed these serial crimes. At the moment, almost everyone in the community was a potential suspect.

But then, another thought occurred to her.

"I have an idea," she said to Owen as they walked away.

"What are you thinking?" he asked.

"I'm wondering - why was Sadie targeted? She was allowed into the post-prom party most likely because she was a dealer."

"Yes, exactly, that's very sad," Owen agreed.

"But she seems to have been very small time. A student dealer? Gets hold of a few sleeves of pills and sells them? She didn't have a huge stash on her, or any seriously hard drugs."

"It seems that way."

May could see from Owen's face that he was following her line of thought. "So, what if there were other dealers there who didn't want her muscling in?"

"Or perhaps other dealers weren't allowed in the party and she was?" May suggested. "That could have created a motive for revenge."

"We definitely need to explore that possibility," Owen agreed. "Anything illegal creates more of a criminal motive, and a big party like that would have attracted those types. They always do. Maybe Alyssa was involved as a customer. She might have bought from Sadie. That would explain why they were both targeted."

May liked Owen's theory that Alyssa, or maybe Dylan, had bought from Sadie. The toxicology results hadn't yet come back for Alyssa, and would probably take another couple of days, so she still didn't know if she had used any drugs or not.

But this presented a definite motive.

They now needed to interview the students again, focusing on the drug element at this out-of-control party, to see if any other dealers were either there or else chased away.

CHAPTER TEN

As May walked back down the path, her phone started ringing and, glancing at the screen, her already-high stress levels escalated.

It was her older sister on the line.

May knew Kerry must be calling to discuss the wedding, and she felt another lurch of fear that she would be asked to be the maid of honor. She just didn't see how she was going to find the time.

This would strain the family dynamics in every possible way, and with May now embroiled in a murder investigation, she simply couldn't take leave from work.

She was just going to have to say no, and face the consequences. She cringed to think of her mother's disappointment, and the sad, yet cutting words she would utter when reprimanding May. It was astonishing, she thought, how just thinking of these family situations could make her feel fifteen years old and helpless, all over again.

She knew she couldn't let herself feel this way, because she was nearly twice that age now, and knew better. She had to try and stand up for herself, while also somehow managing the situation.

"Hey, Kerry," May said, her voice sounding just as friendly and enthusiastic as she could make it. "How are you?"

"I'm well," Kerry said. "I just wanted to touch base with you. Things are so hectic this side that I haven't been able to fly out to do the pre-wedding prep I wanted to. So I'm going to have to delay that trip. We're deeply involved in two very serious cases."

May breathed a sigh of relief.

"I'm about to go into a press conference. But I was wondering." Her voice became low and friendly.

All May's instincts flared as she imagined Kerry, seated at some big, oaken desk in a flashy FBI office, probably with flags on one wall and all her certificates of achievement and bravery on another wall.

Her imagination might be totally wrong. Perhaps Kerry was in some humble, shared office cubicle under a harsh fluorescent light, but the oak-lined office was the direction May's thoughts instinctively went.

"I was wondering, sis, since you're right there and you have the time..."

May felt cold shivers lance down her spine. She didn't have the time! She was absolutely sure this was going to involve an excessive amount of time.

"You know, there are so many beautiful venues in that part of the world. *Our* part of the world," Kerry continued. "There are so many lovely, special places. I have a long, long list all written down."

"What are you thinking?" May asked, her voice rising in pitch.

Kerry chuckled. "I know what you're thinking. Yes, I'm sure your days are also fairly full, but I need to know about the best venues. This isn't something that can wait. After all, they tend to get booked up way in advance. So, I was wondering if you would take a look, not just for me, but for yourself too. After all, you want to enjoy this wedding, right?" Confidence resounded from her voice.

"Wait," May stuttered out.

"What we need to do is reduce the numbers down from the longlist to the shortlist," Kerry continued.

We? May didn't see any 'we' in this endeavor, which Kerry was trying to plant squarely on her shoulders.

"Look, I - " she began.

And then May ran out of courage to stand up to her older sister.

"I have to go. My boss is waiting to talk to me," she muttered, and killed the call, her face flaming from the lie. She hated lying. Why had she even said that? Why hadn't she been brave enough to tell the truth?

As she rushed back to her car, May reminded herself that if she didn't find the courage to stand up to Kerry, this would only get more difficult with every new demand that arrived. In fact, she was already heading for disaster.

*

Back in the car, she and Owen wasted no time. They logged into the case documents, and looked up the list of partygoers which Sheriff Jack had compiled.

"I guess we go alphabetically," May said. She didn't know what else to do.

"Let's hope we can get all of them to talk to us," Owen said. "I mean, it's going to be a lot of work to get a detailed statement from all of them. There must have been close to fifty people there when I arrived. And that's excluding the possibility that the killer ran away as soon as he'd killed."

May sighed. That was a major stumbling block and one that had been haunting her thoughts, too.

"He could have done that. So we also need to ask if they noticed anyone who left suddenly."

"What are the chances we're going to get anyone to talk to us?" Owen pointed out. "The parents are going to start being very protective. I get the idea this is going to turn into a sort of competition. That someone else's kid must take the fall. Especially when we start asking about drugs."

"I think it's going to be really hard," May said. "I guess we'll have to try it and see how we get on."

"Shall we do her first?" Owen asked, pointing to the first name on the list, Amy Sanders.

May looked at the address which Sheriff Jack had jotted down.

"We need to decide," she said. "What are we going to do? Calls or visits? We don't have time to visit everyone, but a visit might be more effective."

Owen frowned.

"Perhaps we can make sense of this list. Let's drop by the first few who are closest, and on the way, and call those who are furthest away."

May thought that was a great idea.

"So we call Amy Sanders, while we head to Paul Maher, who is the closest."

Nodding, Owen dialed Amy's home number. A woman answered.

"I'm looking for Amy Sanders," Owen said.

"I'm sorry, she is asleep. And I am not speaking to any more of you. You journalists are like vultures!"

The phone was slammed down, disconnecting so brusquely that May winced.

"I didn't have time to say anything!" Owen protested. "Should I call back?"

May shook her head. "Let's move on. We can always try her again at the end."

"Well, who's next on the list?" Owen asked worriedly. "I'll try and say we're police, as quick as I can this time."

"Barbie Martins."

Owen dialed the number.

A man answered, his voice sounding gruff and tired.

"Yeah?"

"I'm police. Deputy Owen Lovell calling," Owen gabbled out. "I'm sorry to disturb you, but we're conducting inquiries into a murder investigation. We need to speak to Barbie Martins."

"My daughter? Why? She's resting now."

"Sir, this is a murder inquiry. It's rather urgent."

"Look, I don't want to wake her," the man said. "She's sleeping. She was very sick earlier. She threw up repeatedly and had a hysterical crying fit. She's very upset over what happened to Alyssa. I don't want to disturb her if I can possibly help it, do you know what I mean? Can we do this later? She doesn't know anything, and if I wake her, she'll be really mad at me."

"We'll call again later," Owen said, sounding resigned.

May nodded sympathetically as Owen killed the call. Being a community police officer had its drawbacks. Consideration was expected. After all, the locals didn't have to make pies and cakes when the police did something important to help the area. They did it because it was all about being part of a community.

"Are we going to get anyone to talk to us?" she said.

"Well, we're almost at Paul Maher's house," Owen said. "Turn right here. Hopefully, being outside their door might get us further."

May drove past the house and parked on the side of the road. She didn't feel optimistic at all.

The house was a smallish one on a quiet street. The lawn was neatly cut and there was a fence around the front garden. A camera was mounted on the roof, a sign that the residents were security conscious.

As they walked up to the gate, a short, blonde, round-faced woman opened the door and looked at them quizzically.

"Are you looking for me?" she asked.

"I'm sorry to bother you," Owen said. "We're police. We're conducting an investigation into the death of Alyssa Darlington, who was killed early this morning, and Sadie Croft, who was found dead just now."

The woman clapped her hands over her mouth.

"Two murders?" she whispered. "I didn't know there have been two!"

"Unfortunately, yes. We are just making a preliminary inquiry, but we really do need to ask Paul Maher some questions."

"Come in, please," she said.

Feeling relieved they'd at least gotten inside the house, May followed Owen into the home where the woman led them to a small cozy lounge with navy blue furniture.

"I'll go and fetch him," the woman said.

She hurried out of the room and in a moment came back with a short, blonde, round-faced boy who was clearly her son.

He looked pale and tired, but sat down and gave them an honest stare. Mrs. Maher glanced at him protectively and May felt her stomach sink.

With a stroke of genius, Owen intervened.

"Mrs. Maher?" he asked the blonde.

"Yes. What is it?"

"Could I interview you separately, outside, to save some time?" he said, with a conspiratorial glance at May. "There are just a few background questions I need to discuss."

"Sure. Sure."

She followed him out, to May's relief.

Now, with the parent out of the way thanks to Owen's clever maneuver, she thought Paul would speak more freely.

"I'm sorry about what's happened," she opened up. "We now have two students murdered. Alyssa Darlington, and also Sadie Croft."

She saw his eyebrows shoot up at the second name.

"I was Alyssa's friend at school," he said, his voice shaking.

"We are trying to build a picture of what happened. If you could tell us what you saw, that would be a big help."

"I don't know how much help I can be. I was, sort of, asleep when this all happened," he confessed.

"It's still important to know what you heard and saw," May said. "So you were asleep. Where were you?"

"I was under a tree. I had too much - er - well, I guess, too much to drink."

May looked at him closely. She thought this was a good opportunity to discreetly inquire about the dealer.

"We have heard that there might have been some people there, trying to sell alcohol and drugs."

Already, he was shaking his head vigorously.

"Obviously we are not going to prosecute any witnesses to a murder case for revealing information we need," May said firmly, hoping Paul would get the message.

Now, he looked up, showing interest.

"But we do need to know if there were any known people there, selling illegal substances. Imagine if we were able to find the killer, thanks to somebody being honest? That person would definitely receive our gratitude and respect."

She waited.

Paul shifted his feet.

"You sure I won't get in trouble?"

"I promise you," May reassured him.

"Because you know, my mom's been saying that we really need to catch this killer, that anyone could be next. And I feel bad telling you this, but yes, there was someone there who I had seen before, and know about."

"Who is that person?" May asked, feeling grateful that Paul was willing to speak.

"He - well, I don't know his real name. But everyone calls him Skunk," he said in a low voice.

Skunk? Well, this was a step forward.

"Does he sell drugs to people?"

"Yes. He used to be a student at Higginsvale High, a few years ago. He moves in those circles where he knows a lot of people, and he thinks he can do whatever he wants. Especially if there is money involved."

"And you saw him there?"

"Yes. Some of the guys tried to chase him off. I saw him shouting at Sadie. Saying she was on his turf. There was definitely trouble between them. I saw him pull a knife on one of the other guys but I don't know why. Then I think they surrounded him and he drove off in a hurry."

"What does he look like?" May asked.

"About six foot tall, with long, tangled hair and a scar on his cheek," Paul said.

"Thank you," May said.

With the description, and the school he'd gone to, she was sure that they could now find out exactly who Skunk was, and hopefully track down his whereabouts.

This was exactly the kind of violent man, with an illegal motive, who was likely to have committed such a crime, May thought, feeling encouraged.

CHAPTER ELEVEN

"This sure is the wrong side of the tracks," Owen said in an uncertain voice to May, as she headed down the potholed road that led to the disued railway station adjoining the trailer park.

"Well, it's definitely where Skunk is said to hang out, according to the police reports," May confirmed.

She wished they'd gotten this lead earlier. It was already late afternoon now, and getting dark, and it had taken them nearly an hour to reach this location.

Luckily, Skunk had been well-known to a few of the police departments, especially the ones on this side of Tamarack County, where the town of Higginsvale and Higginsvale High School were located. May had quickly learned that his real name was Ryan Hatcher, and he'd been arrested several times for possession of drugs and illegal firearms.

Now, here they were, at the old railway station, which had been shut down for a long time since the railway line was relocated to a nearby river bridge and the tracks were torn up.

The old railway station had once been a point of pride for the area, but it had long since been abandoned. The windows had been boarded up with plywood, the roof was leaking, and the place had a bad reputation. The town it was in, Goodsville, was one of the poorest in the area, on the far west of Tamarack County.

This was way outside the Fairshore jurisdiction and May hadn't had reason to visit this town more than a couple of times in the past.

She looked around her as they drove through.

The station was in a hollow, which was surrounded by streets of shabby old houses, with patched roofs and broken windows. The potholed roads were surprisingly quiet, although May saw a few people on foot loitering nearby.

"This place has really gone downhill," she said to Owen. "It's such a shame that this station hasn't been renovated or repurposed." As a policewoman, May hated to see the bad parts of town that were always the problematic crime hotspots. She never attended a callout to places like this without wishing that the area could be uplifted and the core problems that had led to the decay, addressed. Her heart ached for the families and children in these less privileged areas.

"Not much opportunity for work here, I guess," Owen said, clearly thinking along the same lines as he looked around with a worried frown. "If you're not in the drug business, that is."

Beyond the station, she saw the trailer park, on a piece of vacant land between the station and a light industrial area, with a few small factories and businesses, including a scrap metal yard, a lumberyard, and an auto parts supplier.

The trailers were bunched together in rows, with a wide gap between each row. The lots were filled with junk cars and trash. May noticed a few people hanging out on the porches of the trailers. The air was filled with smoke.

There was a strong feeling of menace in the air that made May feel a little uneasy.

She knew she was on the right track in asking Skunk questions, but now she was wondering if two of them would be enough. May had a strong sense that in this part of the world, police were not liked or trusted. That was most definitely the impression she was getting.

She parked the car outside the main gateway, which was nothing more than two rusty gateposts set in the ground.

"You ready?" she asked Owen.

He nodded, looking resolute. "Let's go find Skunk," he said.

May glanced again at the ID photo on her phone. Skunk, aka Ryan Hatcher, was twenty-three years old, a tall, stringy man with limp, straggly brown hair that seemed to adhere to his narrow head, and a shifty look in his eyes. The scar, on his left cheek, was very distinctive.

May got his features in her mind. Then, with her chin up, she walked over the potholed road and into the trailer park.

She stopped at the first trailer, which had a man and woman sitting outside. The trailer had a cracked wooden fence around it, and a rusted old car was parked in the front yard.

"Good evening. We're looking to speak to Ryan Hatcher. Do you know if he's here anywhere?"

The couple on the plastic chairs looked sullen, and they didn't move. The woman shook her head in silence.

A few of the younger children, however, peeked out of the windows of the trailer, entranced by the sight of the uniformed police officers.

A woman peered out of a nearby trailer, and frowned at them.

"Who you looking for?" she called out in a suspicious voice. She was a thin woman with a pinched face. "It's late. What do you want this time of day?"

May showed her the picture of Skunk.

"This man is wanted for questioning in a murder case," she said. "We were told he's probably here."

"What about it?" the woman asked suspiciously. "I don't know where he is."

"Maybe you can tell us which one of these trailers is his?" May asked.

"I don't know. I'm not his mother," she retorted.

A man in a Harley T-shirt peered out of the window of the trailer at the end of the row. His head was shaven, and he had a huge silver hoop in his ear.

"Do you know the whereabouts of Ryan Hatcher, known as Skunk?" May asked him.

He shrugged. "Nope," he said casually.

May walked on, determined that Skunk could not hide away forever.

"This man is wanted for questioning in a murder case," May said, showing a group of people sitting on a porch a photograph of Skunk on her phone. "We were told he's probably here."

There was a glimmer of interest in at least one pair of eyes, and a few of the others turned their heads to look at her.

The man who was sitting on the porch, smoking, laughed.

"Everyone knows Skunk around here," he said.

"How would I find him? Is he here?" she asked.

"He was here earlier, but now I'm not sure where he disappeared to," the man said, showing his yellow teeth in a grin. "He comes and goes all the time, so if he's not here, he'll be back soon."

May felt encouraged that they were, at least, were getting close.

"Which is his trailer?" she asked.

The man shrugged. "One of the trailers near the end, I guess."

"You can't say more?"

The man shrugged, grinning.

"I don't know. I'd be careful if I were you. Skunk has a bad temper, and he hates cops."

May walked in the direction he'd indicated, but the last three trailers in the row were empty and unlit. She saw no one she could ask, and the trailers nearby were all quiet.

Darkness was falling quickly, and the park was taking on a more sinister look.

Just as she turned away from the last trailer, she spotted a man hunched, speaking on his phone, in a dusty old car. It was an old red Chevy, parked at the end of the lot.

May recognized the man, who was sitting behind the steering wheel. She could see the scar, and that lanky hair.

"It's Skunk!" she whispered to Owen. Undoubtedly this was the man they were seeking. They'd found him at last.

May hurried over to the Chevy.

Skunk was sitting in the driver's seat, his head turned away from her, as he spoke on the phone.

She could see he was talking to someone, giving rapid instructions. But, as she approached, Skunk looked up and saw her.

He stared incredulously at her, taking in who she was, and Owen's presence as he walked in front of the car to prevent Skunk from driving away.

Then, he did something they hadn't expected. He yanked open the car door with a scream of hinges, jumped out, and took off running as fast as he could.

CHAPTER TWELVE

"Hey! Stop! We're the police!" May yelled at the fleeing dealer. Of course, Skunk ignored her, zigzagging at top speed along the dusty roads that led through the trailer park.

His skinny legs looked like they were going to fly off his body, but he was fast, and May was struggling to keep up.

He didn't look like a man who would go down easily, and she was glad that Owen was there to help her. For a start, he had more chance of keeping pace with this fast-moving criminal. But so far, Owen hadn't even caught up with her. Where was he? There was no time to look for where he'd gone, because if she did, she'd lose sight of her suspect. She could only hope that Owen was calling for backup, or doing something else that would save the situation.

Skunk darted through the gateposts and into the street, trying to get away from her. His demeanor was panicked and he was keeping his head low.

Cries of encouragement, jeers, curses and catcalls filtered into the dusty air from the trailer park that was now behind them. Clearly, the residents had mixed feelings about this chase, but all had an opinion.

May's only focus was on catching up with this dealer, who could well be the killer they were hunting.

He clearly knew the area well. He dodged down an alleyway leading through a broken building, that had narrow passages branching from it. The alleyway was littered with cigarette butts, and stank of urine.

The walls were covered in graffiti, and broken glass crunched underfoot as May plowed through the passageway after him.

Which way had he turned? For a heart-stopping moment, she thought she'd lost him.

The pounding of footsteps clued her in. She veered down the nearest cross-passage and followed him at top speed.

Then, suddenly, they were out of the ruined building, and Skunk began running along a wide, open road. On one side was a vacant, littered plot of ground that led into the back of the trailer park, and on the other was a warehouse and a junkyard. It was so dark now that she could barely see him. He was little more than a shadowy figure in the gloom.

Ahead of them gleamed a low-slung, metal fence that Skunk vaulted over as if he were a gymnast.

May ran as fast as she could and let out a cry as she vaulted after him. The fence was about five feet high, and she managed to grab the top with both hands and fling herself over, using her speed to propel herself upward, landing on the other side with a thump.

Skunk had gained a little distance on her, and was running as fast as he could along the fence line. May's heart sank. She couldn't keep up this pace for much longer. Skunk was either powered by adrenaline, or else some other probably illegal substance.

Was she going to lose him? she wondered with a flare of fear as the distance slowly, inexorably widened.

And where was Owen? She hoped nothing had happened to him.

Then, suddenly, May saw what he'd been up to.

As soon as he had seen which way Skunk was headed, it looked like her deputy must have doubled back and run through the trailer park itself. His strategy had worked.

Now, the thud of footsteps clued her in, and she recognized his tall silhouette. He was racing toward Skunk from the other direction.

Skunk couldn't get away – he was trapped between the two officers.

The fence line was coming to an end. Veering desperately to the right, Skunk turned and started running across the junkyard. But they had him boxed in, and there was nowhere for him to go.

Skunk started running straight for a pile of garbage that was heaped up on the other side of the fence. He looked as if he was going to try to scramble over it.

"Stop! Police!" Owen shouted, in a voice that carried over the distance. "If you try to climb that pile, I will shoot!"

But Skunk leaped for the pile.

Owen was close behind him now. He dove for the man's leg and managed to grab hold of it.

May could see Skunk kicking out at him, and she could hear her partner grunting with the effort.

Then Skunk fell back with a scream, and the two of them tumbled down the pile of junk together. Metal clanged and cans clattered as they rolled together on the floor.

"Get off! Get off me!" Skunk shrieked.

May leaped forward and grabbed his arm, holding on as hard as she could.

Skunk tried to wrench his arm free, but he couldn't do it, and May was glad that Owen now had a firm hold of his other arm, and was dragging it behind the dealer's back.

The click of the handcuffs sounded loud in the silence.

Skunk was breathing in great, rasping gulps, and she could see he was exhausted.

He turned to look over his shoulder at Owen and May. He let out a vicious curse.

"You're coming in to the police department," May told him breathlessly but triumphantly. "We need to question you in connection with two recent murders."

*

Half an hour later, May stood outside the interview room, ready to question Skunk. Her nerves were still jangling after that chase. If he'd gotten away, if he'd managed to vanish into the gloom, they'd never have caught him.

And now it was fully dark.

"You were brilliant taking that shortcut," she told Owen.

He nodded modestly. "I remembered being called out to that area a few months ago, and I had a good idea of the layout. I'm just lucky he chose to run that way," he said.

"Well, let's see if we carry on being lucky and he confesses," May said.

Although, as she stepped inside the interview room, she knew this part of the investigation rested solely on her shoulders. There was no more luck involved. Skill and thoroughness would get her where she wanted to be.

Drawing on her control and resolve, May stepped into the room with Owen following her.

Skunk glared at them. He didn't look any friendlier in the harsh light of the interview room. In fact, May thought, it accentuated his frown lines as he met her eyes.

"Ryan Hatcher," she said firmly.

"What is it?" Skunk snapped.

May took a deep breath. She had no doubt that this man was a drug dealer. What she didn't know was whether he was a killer. She had to make him realize he was cornered, and there was no point in him denying the full truth anymore.

"We have evidence that you have been dealing drugs in this area, and particularly, that you were seen at a post-prom party at the Hazelwood Pavilion last night," May said.

Skunk blinked. "Not me," he said reflexively.

"Can you confirm your whereabouts last night?" May asked calmly.

Skunk looked at the floor. "Er," he said. "I was at home."

"Witnesses saw you at the party. I believe the term 'chased off' was used. Is that your Chevy? If so, you do know we can check camera footage on all available observation points. There are several between the trailer park and the venue. I'm sure if we search, we might pick you up. Of course if we find you have been lying to us, it won't go well for you at all. Didn't you just get out of jail recently? I'm pretty sure you got out of jail not too long ago."

"You wouldn't want to go back, would you?" Owen added.

"I - I swear, man, I'm clean. Did you find any drugs on me?" Skunk asked innocently.

May was sure he'd dumped them in the Chevy before leading them on that chase.

"You went there to sell drugs," May insisted. "You went there to sell drugs, and then things went wrong. Perhaps you perceived that the second victim was treading on your turf?"

Skunk's mouth fell open.

"Wait, what? You mean that misfit type woman, what's her name, Sadie? Someone killed her?" He sounded incredulous. "No, man, that's not right. She never deserved it! Look, I know she was selling pills but I wasn't going to give her a hard time about it. She buys from me, too. Or has. Or rather, did. Yeah, I said she was on my turf, but we knew where we stood with each other. I was just trying to show the other guys that I was tough and they needed to stop hounding me away."

He looked horrified, as if he'd just given far too much information away in that brief, shocked outburst.

May considered his words. Helpful as they were, this wasn't the reaction she'd expected from him.

"Where were you in the early hours of the morning, onward? Do you have an alibi at all for any time of this day? And I want the truth!" she threatened.

Skunk sighed.

"I got chased away from the party at about two a.m. I didn't stick around, man. I went through to a nightclub and sold some stuff there. I even saw one of the guys there. Name of Miles. You ask him, we know each other. He was there with some good looking girl. And then at seven a.m. I reported for my parole check-in. The officer wasn't there so I had to wait a couple hours until he arrived. The times are all recorded. I left there at about ten-thirty."

He spread his arms, staring innocently at May.

She nodded, feeling surprised that his version had, in fact, added up.

He could not have been the killer, even though May was still going to double check his alibi and also planned to hold him on drug dealing charges. But as far as these murders went, they were going to have to go back to the drawing board. This lack of suspects was deeply concerning. It was now night time, and they still had no idea who the perpetrator was.

They had two victims, who had attended the same school.

May decided that she now had to draw on the common threads between these two girls. There must be some. There had to be a reason why these two, out of many, were deliberately targeted. May knew she had to dig into those potential reasons. If she pulled on the right thread, she hoped it would lead her further in the search.

CHAPTER THIRTEEN

The girls were ripe for the picking. Prom night was over. He'd waited so patiently, he knew. How he'd controlled himself. Patience reaped its own rewards.

The teacher smiled as he thought about it. What pleasure there had been in finally getting close to his objects of desire.

Two beautiful girls. Among the most beautiful in the class, he thought. His own personal first and second princesses. His own idols of the prom.

He hadn't taken them until they were ready. But he knew prom night meant they were ready.

They were women now, and they could be his. And yet, they had rejected him. He'd seen it in their eyes.

It was unfortunate they had to die as a result. He knew that was very sad. He'd felt a deep pang of guilt when he'd taken the first one.

But then he'd reminded himself that she'd led him on. Her lips, her eyes, her beautiful hair had all been a clear invitation, even though she hadn't known it. She'd led him on and then, heartlessly, caused him grief by ignoring him.

Hovering around them at school, he'd watched as they flirted. Laughing, tilting their heads, playing with their hair, they'd sent out the signals he was waiting for. But not to him, even though he'd noticed every one.

He had even followed them home, careful to stay out of sight. He had taken many pictures of them, just to freeze the moments in time.

They would forever live in his memory. He felt he had captured their essence.

This way, they would always be his. It was a more beautiful ending, perhaps the perfect ending to their lives.

He had known what was going to happen and that gave the teacher a warm feeling that was like the very best kind of head rush. He closed his eyes, and he recalled the moments that he'd watched them, knowing they were his, and always would be.

With pride in his heart, but sadness, too, he'd watched them dance at the prom, both of them, in the flashes of strobe light. He'd watched them in the darkness of the night, walking over the moist grass, in the moonlight.

And in his heart he'd felt a surge of regret that neither of them looked at him the same way. Oh, no. They reserved all their attention, all their charms, for those stupid, juvenile boys.

But he was something special. He was better than those boys. He was older, and he knew what he was doing.

After all, he was a man, while those boys were nothing more than children.

He'd felt a rage at that, and it had festered until the feeling had become too much. He'd crushed the feeling down, and he'd waited. They had chosen their own fate. It was their fault that they'd angered him and caused him to have to do what he did.

He'd watched them; then he'd taken them.

He'd done it respectfully. Cleanly. And he had paid them the ultimate courtesy. He hadn't looked into their eyes at the moment they died. He thought that was a sign of his reverence for them. Only afterward had he laid them down on the ground and stared at their dead faces.

He'd strewn them with petals, a sign of his love and admiration for his prom princesses, a reflection of their own beauty. The petals had been stripped from the flowers, just as they had been stripped from their life. Flowers and women, combined to create the perfect sacrificial scenario, he thought, pleased with his logic.

And of course, he was careful to leave nothing behind. No evidence. No witnesses.

Nobody would ever know what he did outside of school hours. Except for them. He'd allowed each of them to see what lurked within him before the final chase, because he had felt it important, that they needed to know. He'd trusted them with his ultimate secret. How lucky they were!

His heart was pounding as he turned off the road, onto the timber plantation. It was the pine trees, he thought. The scent of pine, which had always made him feel so energized, and so happy.

These moments, so special to him, could not possibly stop. Not until he had taken his final prize. Three was a lucky number. Three was the total he needed.

The third girl he planned to take was very special to him. While the other two were the first and second princesses, she was his prom queen. That was how he thought of her.

She was a soft, vulnerable soul. Not as obviously beautiful as the other two, but he saw her attraction. Those soft eyes, that incredible figure. Hair like silk.

She hadn't paid him any attention, so he was going to take her life as well. What a privilege it would be to get so close to this beautiful woman, and to share her last moments on earth, even though she had rejected him and he knew there could never be more between them.

What would she see? What would she feel?

He knew she would see him, and she would feel him. And then she would be gone.

She was so special to him, so beautiful. He could feel the aftermath of the ecstasy already. The warm feelings, the head rush.

Bemused, the teacher realized that this experience was like a drug to him now. The moments when they saw him standing and watching would forever be engraved in his mind. He wanted to relieve the clench of his heart that he felt as he watched their faces change, with terror and fear written over those beautiful features.

He had made such an impression on them. For the first time they had seen, really seen him. Now, soon, his prom queen would do the same. She would see him for who he was. Not who he pretended to be.

But first, he had to get to her, and he knew he had to do it fast. They would be locking down the community. They would be searching for suspects. But he thought he was ahead of them. He was sure the local police would not move fast. County sheriffs. Not such a high caliber of investigator, surely? Slow, rural and bumbling, he guessed. He was confident he had the time to do what he craved, and then to cover his tracks.

Getting to her. How could that be done in the way that would suit him best? This girl had few hobbies. She wasn't a rebel. She didn't go out running alone. She didn't have a boyfriend to sneak out into the woods with.

So this would be more difficult, a challenge for him.

The teacher considered it. He liked a challenge. It was all part of the chase. It was the pressure of time that made it more difficult. By tomorrow morning, at the latest, he wanted to have this underway.

Luckily he had been observing this girl and he thought there was one solution that would work perfectly.

It was so easy to watch her, to watch all of them, from behind the darkened windows of the utterly average car he drove. A car nobody noticed, in a color the eyes slipped over.

He was good at that. Watching. Staying unseen. And he had an extremely sharp eye for detail, which had served him well many times.

The teacher was good at many things.

The teacher knew he was good at murder. And getting better with each new girl he took.

Although the police were involved, he knew, for sure, that nobody would ever find him out.

The teacher was always very careful to leave no traces.

He parked the car, and then got out into the cool, spring night. He looked up at the sky.

There was no moon. He liked that. And tomorrow morning was supposed to start off cool but fine. Again, what he needed. The elements were working in his favor.

He walked along the path, thinking of how he was going to manage his next and final sacrifice. It would be his last one, so he needed to make sure it got done in a way that would leave an even bigger impact and memory, seared in his soul.

Humming softly, he mused over his plans as he strolled.

CHAPTER FOURTEEN

May wasn't going to allow herself to panic. She reminded herself firmly of that. No panic. Even though it was now late at night, and all their suspects had checked out, and they were now back to doing the most basic groundwork in the hope that something they had missed became glaringly obvious.

Sighing, she turned back to her work.

Her first task was to identify the similarities between the two victims.

May had gathered a host of resources at her disposal. She had the school yearbooks which she'd looked up online, as well as the curriculums and the classes each one had attended. Sheriff Jack had contacted the school principal who had provided the info while she and Owen were on their way back.

Now it was up to May herself to connect the dots.

Sadie and Alyssa. Her heart contracted as she thought about them. Two beautiful girls, their lives cut short, their families devastated.

But what, apart from attending the same school, did they have in common?

May went through the yearbook with a fine-tooth comb. Alyssa had been a cheerleader, on the school paper, runner up in Miss Popularity. She'd achieved two academic awards.

Sadie seemed to have been a total rebel. She'd avoided anything and everything. She had been scraping by with grades only a few marks above flunking.

They didn't have any friends in common or any activities in common that May could see. And that wasn't surprising, she acknowledged, with a resigned shake of her head. They didn't have much in common at all, apart from both being particularly beautiful.

At that moment, Owen walked in, carrying a box of pizza.

"Oh, thank you," May said, grabbing a slice and digging in gratefully. She was starving. The crispy crust, spicy pepperoni and gooey, hot cheese tasted delicious.

"Have you found anything?" Owen asked. "Because to be honest, I haven't. Not really."

May shook her head.

"There seems to be very little intersection between them. But maybe we're looking into this too deeply."

Munching a slice of his own pizza, Owen raised his eyebrows.

"How do you mean?" he asked.

"Maybe it's not where they intersected. Maybe it's just that they both happened to have a connection with the wrong person. A bad person. It could be that simple. They both came into frequent contact with a psychopath who targeted them. And that would surely mean it was someone who worked at the school."

"That's possible, I guess." Owen grabbed another slice and pushed the box across to May. She did the same.

"Some of the teachers taught across all the grades. Core subjects, you know? English, math, and so on. But the victims didn't share classes. As far as I can see from this curriculum there's only one class they had in common, that they both attended at the same time."

"What's that?" Owen asked.

"It was PE. For that subject, they went according to gender, not to class. And they were able to choose their activities."

"Ah." Owen said.

"They were divided into teams, and here I see Alyssa and Sadie were on the same team. This team played hockey and it was taught by Coach Adamson."

"Okay," Owen said. "So it's likely that both Sadie and Alyssa interacted frequently with Adamson."

"And at the same time," May said. "In fact, they were both in his special sports coaching class according to the curriculum here. A by-invitation-only class. Maybe that should be our starting point. We have to start somewhere, and he seems the strongest link."

"So what do we know about Coach Adamson?" Owen asked.

"We know he teaches football, hockey, gymnastics and athletics. He has been at the school for, let me see - for four years according to this list."

"And what other details do you have?"

"He's thirty-eight years old and lives in Floral Ridge, which is about ten miles from the school."

Now May could see that Owen was energized by the job of doing research.

"Okay. I'm going to have a look at his home address and background. Let's find out a little more about him. If anything stands out, we can always contact the Floral Ridge police and ask if he's ever been in any trouble."

While Owen bent to his task, working between two different laptops, May grabbed a third slice of pizza. Finally, this was starting to fill the hole from not eating all day.

Then she, too, joined him, typing in the information, checking out the comparisons, searching with an eagle eye to find out if there was anything at all irregular that might point them in the direction of investigating Coach Adamson further. Once they had checked him out thoroughly, May decided, they could go on to the others. If nobody rang any alarm bells, she guessed they would need to make a personal visit to the school and interview every single staff member, checking their whereabouts and potential alibis.

They worked in silence, quietly and efficiently. May was aware of the sound of their breathing - the only sound in the room apart from the clacking of keyboards and the regular rustle of the pizza box.

There were no speeding tickets, no parking fines, nothing. If anything, Adamson was a little too clean.

But maybe, May thought, he was clean for a reason. Maybe something had happened long ago that had caused him to try and become a reformed character. Maybe he'd done that, but now his demons were surfacing again?

The thought enthused her. That could be a real possibility. And it was fairly easy to search. She'd done it before.

Frowning, May corrected herself as she tried. It had been easy to search last time. What was going on? Was she doing it wrong this time?

After jumping back and forth between the databases, May gave a frustrated sigh.

"This is weird."

"What's weird?" Owen asked.

"I think I'm doing this wrong. I was looking for older background, and I can't seem to find anything on this coach going back more than about eight years. I've looked in other databases. There's nothing to be found. Is your system online?"

May wondered if hers was offline or hiccupping.

"Mine is online, yes." Owen looked closer, tapping more keys. "I'm going in now, too. It was clever of you to think of doing that, May. Sometimes older records can be very helpful."

There was silence except for the click of the keyboard.

"There's nothing. I mean, I'm looking everywhere now. Every database. Now this system is going really slow," May complained.

Owen stuffed the last of the pizza into his mouth.

"It's slow but it's working, and it's telling me that this guy didn't seem to move from anywhere. He just appeared. Eight years ago, he materialized in Tamarack County, and got a job at a junior high school. From there, he moved to the school where he is now."

"Nothing beyond that?"

Owen seemed hell bent on his mission now.

"Okay, I'll switch to another system. Maybe I can find something on him there?" He paused. "I'm in. I see the correct screen, May. Look, I've found him. Finally! But there's no information on him."

He leaned back in his chair, rubbing his forehead, and then glared once again at the screen.

"We have to try and research this further," May said.

"How are we going to do that?"

May felt a sense of doom descend. She could think of only one way to do it.

This was a really, really bad time. In fact, it could not be a worse time. If she did this, she was going to owe Kerry big time, at a moment in her life when Kerry wanted her to spend an undetermined, but extraordinary number of hours personally researching hundreds of venues dotted all over Tamarack County.

And yet, the might of the FBI could open doors in a flash, where the local sheriff's department would be knocking forever.

"I'm going to have to call my sister," May said, feeling as if fate was really not working with her here in terms of timing. "She might be able to tell us."

Owen's face lit up.

"What a great idea," he said. "Do you think she'll pick up if we call her now?"

CHAPTER FIFTEEN

May walked outside to make the call to Kerry. She feared it would be difficult to navigate this conversation without disaster, and she needed fresh air. It felt like she'd been sitting at that desk for hours. Checking the time, she saw she had, in fact, been sitting at that desk for hours.

No wonder her neck was stiff and her eyes felt scratchy. Breathing in the cool, breezy night air, she dialed Kerry's number.

Her sister picked up on the third ring.

"Hey, sis."

"Hi, Kerry. I'm sorry to call you so late. Is this a good moment?"

"Late?" Kerry laughed. "I'm just heading back to the office now after a highly successful takedown. Two drug kingpins will be behind bars for a long, long time. I have a couple hours of paperwork ahead. Then I might think about a bite to eat."

She sounded as fresh as if she'd just gotten out of bed, and now guilty thoughts of her own pizza were weighing on May's mind. She was sure Kerry would have some kind of healthy low carb snack for dinner, involving free range protein and micro herbs. That was the kind of person she was. May still felt as if she had pepperoni stuck in her teeth.

"I have a favor to ask," May began. "I need to talk to you about something. I just don't know if this is the right time."

"Hey, wait! We didn't finish our discussion earlier," Kerry said, as if she'd only just remembered its urgency. "Those venues. I meant to call you back about what I need from you, but honestly, planning this wedding and juggling so many serious cases is a nightmare."

May felt as if she had an insurmountable task ahead. How on earth was she going to refuse to do the impossible, while also asking her sister for an important favor? She loved Kerry. She wanted to be involved in the wedding, and help wherever she could. But she just couldn't do this. It was too big a job. Enthused by the planning, Kerry didn't realize how unreasonable she was being. She needed to turn down this request and do so in a way that didn't hurt or worse still, enrage, Kerry.

She felt as if she'd used up all her tactical skill interviewing Skunk, and had none left. And that interview hadn't done anything other than rule him out as a suspect.

Suddenly, in a flash of brilliance, May came up with an angle that she hoped might save her.

"You know, sis, this is difficult for me to say," she started.

"What do you mean?" Kerry sounded as defensive as she'd known she would.

"You see, I know why you want me to do this. Because you and I are very similar, we'll do it quick, we'll look at the same attributes. But you're ignoring the fact that if we do it this way, we're going to be making the wrong decision."

"And why?" Now Kerry sounded more curious.

"Because you're going to be breaking Mom's heart. I know you don't want that and nor do I."

"Huh?" Now Kerry sounded stunned. "What do you mean?"

"I mean that Mom is so invested in this wedding. And she's so keen to do whatever she can to help. I know this is a big job, but maybe you would trust her with it? She's just so excited about it every step of the way. So longing to get involved. And this would be something she could do easily. She could narrow down the most suitable venues. Imagine what fun she would have. You remember from our family vacations how she loves looking around and seeing every different room in a hotel, and quizzing people about every little detail? That's probably where we both learned some of our interrogation skills from! And then, when she's done that, I could make the final choice, or hopefully even we two could do that together. I'm so keen to help out. But this job is really made for Mom. I can tell you that, now."

May waited, feeling breathless, to see if Kerry had taken the bait.

"Gosh, May, you know, that's a great idea," Kerry said. "I never really thought of Mom doing it. I guess I've always thought of her as holding the fort at home, but it might be really exciting for her."

"You know, you've been wanting to upgrade their car for a while, and they've been refusing. This is your chance to do it, saying they need a newer car for these trips."

"Hey, now that's a clever angle," Kerry said, sounding impressed.

"You could maybe even put her and Dad up for the night at a few of the more remote places. Then they'd be having mini vacations while doing the work. It would be so special for them. Making memories while being involved in your wedding," May added, now feeling she was on a streak of genius, and wishing she hadn't saved all her brilliant ideas for while she was talking to Kerry. If only she'd had them earlier on, while she was investigating this murder.

"That's a great, great idea. You know, I'm so thrilled about this."

May felt relief wash through her.

"Glad you think so," she said.

"I'll call her as soon as I get into the office. I think it's a fantastic solution. What a personal way to involve her. Well, sis, I'm almost at the office so I'd better get going now."

Clearly, Kerry had forgotten all about the favor she, May, had requested.

"Wait!" May yelled.

"What?"

"I need a favor from you! That's why I called!"

"What's that?" Now Kerry sounded impatient. "You know I'm really busy. There's so much going on."

"Do you think you could look into a background check for me?"

There was silence on the other end of the line.

"You want me to do a background check on someone?" Kerry's voice was wary. "Why?"

"This is confidential." May dropped her voice. "We have a suspect. We've been searching for background on him and we just can't find anything. He arrived in Tamarack County eight years ago, and before that, it's as if he didn't exist."

"Seriously?"

"He doesn't seem to have any kind of past whatsoever."

Kerry sighed. "Have you searched properly?"

May felt a flash of irritation. But she subdued it quickly. Her sister was a perfectionist who thought she could do everything better than everyone else, and since she'd been that way all her life, there was no point in getting mad about it now.

"Yes. Both Owen and I have searched every available database. I searched his social security number and the database came up with nothing prior. I searched the national criminal database, and it came up with nothing prior. I even searched government records. No background. It's like he appeared out of nowhere."

"That is weird," Kerry acknowledged.

"I even went over to the jail database, and looked at the criminal records there. He doesn't exist there, either. And it's a murder investigation, Kerry. If this guy has any history, or there's anything irregular in his past, we really need to know."

"Well, it sure sounds like there is something very untoward here."

"I have a feeling it's something bad, and I'm afraid he might be a danger to the community."

"Okay," Kerry said, in a voice so quiet, May wasn't sure she'd even heard her. "I could do it. What's his name?"

"Coach Adamson. His first name is Graeme. Graeme Adamson. He's a PE teacher at the Sleepy Hollow school, and he currently resides at 4 Boardwalk Street in Floral Ridge."

"All right, I'll do that for you. I might have to make a few calls to get it done. But I promise I'll find out as much as I can."

"I really appreciate it," May said.

"Goodnight, sis! I'll talk to you soon!"

The line went dead.

As if she'd had a dose of caffeine or something, May felt energized by the conversation she'd had with Kerry.

Kerry was going to do her this important favor. And she'd managed to keep their relationship intact, and persuade Kerry to choose someone more suitable for the venues job in a way that hadn't hurt her and still left the door open for May to be involved in other, more manageable, ways.

May was hugely relieved that they would soon have the background they needed on Coach Adamson, and know if he was a suspect they needed to pursue.

Instinctively, she sensed there was something highly irregular about this glaring gap in his history. She couldn't wait to hear what Kerry uncovered.

CHAPTER SIXTEEN

May walked back into the police department, feeling encouraged.

"Hey, Owen," she said. "Guess what?"

"What?" he asked, picking up instantly on her excitement.

"Kerry is going to help us. She's going to do the background check on Coach Adamson. I don't know when, but she's a fast worker. She seemed intrigued by it."

"That's great," Owen said. "It was a genius move to ask her for that favor, May. I know that will get us a lot further in the case. I have a feeling about him."

"Me, too," May said.

Owen checked his watch.

"I guess we're done here," he said. "There's not much else we can do now while we're waiting, and it's been a very long day. We can't start calling or interviewing anyone else at this hour, especially not since it seems we should be focusing on Adamson first."

"It has been a long day," May said. Given their predawn start, it was no wonder she was starting to feel as if she'd hit a wall in her thinking. And with a stomach full of pizza, her body was demanding some time out to rest.

"I was wondering."

May glanced at Owen in surprise, because he was sounding extremely nervous. Had he come up with a new theory in the case he was worried about sharing?

"I was wondering, May, if we should maybe drop by Dan's Bar quickly?"

Her deputy was fidgeting uneasily. Something was definitely up.

"You think there's something he might know? A reason for going there?"

May felt immediately uneasy about the thought of venturing into that surprisingly sophisticated local drinking hole that was a meeting spot for the town.

She'd long had a crush on the handsome, suave, well-groomed owner, Dan. And she was now doing her utmost to get over it. She'd realized - well, she strongly suspected - that the crush was unrequited and that her unspoken feelings for Dan were most likely never going to be returned.

Worse still, Dan had long had a crush on her sister, Kerry. Since Kerry had gotten engaged, May had felt as if Dan was exuding hurt and angst every time she went in there.

It was almost as if he perceived her, May, to have personally arranged the betrothal to spite him, when all she'd actually done was tell him about it.

But with everything being so complicated, Dan's Bar wasn't something she could face right now.

"I thought you might like to have a drink there," Owen continued. "It would be good to - to chat about a few other things. Take our mind off the case. I'd like to get to - "

With her mind now latched onto the problematic complexity of Dan, Kerry, and life in general, May shook her head, barely hearing his words.

"I really need to get some rest," she said, in tones that came out sharper than she'd intended.

"Some rest?" A multitude of emotions flickered over Owen's face. Some of them, May couldn't read. She tried her best to clarify.

"I mean, I need to go to bed. I need some sleep. I'm exhausted."

"Oh." Owen looked as if he was going to say something else, but he stopped.

"Don't worry," she tried to reassure him. "We're getting to the core of this case. I know it. It will all come together tomorrow, I'm sure of it."

Owen was staring at her as if he was deeply troubled. Was she missing something? May thought.

"Are you alright?" she asked Owen.

"I just," he began, but then he stopped.

May sensed he was even more disturbed now, but she didn't have the energy to think too much about it. She was bone weary, and her brain was fried. After several long, awkward seconds of silence, Owen stood up and abruptly left the room.

As he shut the door behind him, May sighed. Was he mad at her? Had she said something wrong?

She looked down at her notes.

And then she looked up, letting out a gasp.

Now she saw what this was about! She couldn't believe she'd been such a klutz. She'd totally missed out on the nuances of what he was saying. Now that she thought about it, he'd been hinting at it during their earlier car ride also, when he'd mentioned the art gallery.

May felt her face burning crimson. How could she have been so completely insensitive to what he was asking? It was just that it had been so long since anyone at all had asked her out on a date. That was what it was. A date. She'd forgotten what it was like. Between the case and her sister's wedding, her mind had been utterly distracted.

May buried her hot face in her hands.

This day had twisted around to a disastrous end. She'd managed to totally mess up the situation and had probably wounded Owen by rejecting his offer. In fact, she'd blown it. She'd been too slow. Too slow to understand. Too slow to try to fix things with Owen.

What was she thinking?

And she'd done it in such a blunt way. Really, her behavior had been inexcusable and without any sensitivity. The fact that she hadn't understood the situation was not a mitigating factor.

This could even affect their working relationship. She'd ruined their friendly, easy, companionable vibe, too. How had she managed that? And why? She couldn't even explain it to herself.

Her throat felt hot, tight.

The way he'd started up his car and roared off sounded hurt and angry. May felt her heart sink as low as her self esteem. In her daydreams, she'd never imagined that Owen would ask her out.

Really ask her out.

She'd never thought of him that way. It had just never occurred to her because she'd been so focused on work, during work hours. But yet, now that she played their conversations back in her mind, May realized that they did think along the same lines most times. They were fully in tune with each other. They'd gotten pretty close while working together. They made a damned good team. She liked him a lot. She trusted him.

Never had she imagined that she'd turn him down so hurtfully. And he'd sounded so upset.

Should she call him?

But what would she say? May couldn't think of a thing to say in this situation. It might be too soon. It might be better to leave things be, and see how she felt in the morning. Maybe by then, things would magically seem better.

Or worse, a little voice inside her suggested.

May looked at her watch.

It was close to ten o'clock. It was time to leave, having messed up her closest interpersonal relationship in a most destructive way.

She picked up her purse, turned out the light, and trailed out of the back office to the parking lot.

What would she have done if she had understood what he meant?

That thought gave her a sudden jolt. Would she have said yes to a date? The idea appealed to her in a way. But it also scared her.

Mostly, she realized, because it meant change. And change meant risk. It was safer and more comfortable to keep things as they were.

But it was too late to wonder about that now. She should, instead, be thinking about how she could fix it, and what she was going to say to Owen next time she saw him, tomorrow.

She wasn't sure what it would be like working with him on the case, with this awkwardness and embarrassment now raging through her.

She'd have to try, and hopefully she'd manage. But if she could only have replayed those last few words to him, how differently she would have done things on the second try.

She climbed into her cruiser, fished her keys out of her purse and turned on the ignition.

The engine kicked over.

May drove home thoughtfully, wondering how on earth she could repair the mess she'd made, or whether she'd never again be close to her loyal, clever, and very cute case partner.

And meanwhile, the killer was roaming the county. He'd killed at night before, and she felt terrified that he was planning to kill again. She hoped that Kerry would provide answers as soon as possible that would lead them closer to who he was.

CHAPTER SEVENTEEN

May jerked awake in the semi-darkness, gasping for breath, her arms flailing as she fought off the killer trying to drag her away.

Clutching the bedcovers, gradually, reality filtered back to her.

She'd had a nightmare about Lauren again, after finally managing to sleep. Despite being so tired, she'd tossed and turned, feeling haunted by her life decisions. Now it was getting light on what looked to be a cool but clear day.

Glancing at her alarm clock, she saw it was a quarter to six in the morning.

She might as well start her day, she thought, because she was sure she wouldn't be able to sleep anymore. She felt emotionally wrung out. The debacle with Owen still burned at her when she thought about it.

Why hadn't she given a better answer?

What even was a better answer? She felt so confused. And her eyes felt red, tired, and grainy.

Climbing out of bed, she ran a brush through her hair and then splashed water on her face. Then she went through to the kitchen and put coffee on, making it extra strong in the hope it would magically empower her to feel more awake, and less red-eyed and exhausted.

As she got the machine going, she heard the trill of her phone from the bedroom.

May's heart all but stopped.

A call this early?

It could only be the news she was dreading. Had a third victim been found? With her heart in her mouth, she skidded back into the bedroom and grabbed her phone.

She saw, to her astonishment, it was Kerry.

"Hello?" she answered. Her voice sounded hoarse.

"Morning, sis! Did I wake you?" Kerry sounded amused. There was noise in the background. A repetitive thudding sound and the clink of what sounded like weights.

May realized blearily that her sister must already be at the gym.

Did she need no sleep? Was she superior to May, who needed a full eight hours to function normally, in that way too?

"I was already awake," she mumbled, heading back to the kitchen to pour the coffee.

"Ah, good. I thought I'd better call you now as I'm not sure when I'll have another gap in our day. I'm gymming early. Treadmill, weights, and then we're getting on a helicopter to go track down a rogue witness," Kerry sounded enthused.

"Um, good luck," May said.

She wasn't sure what the take-home message was for her, but she could see that she compared unfavorably to Kerry's work ethic and energy levels. She felt inferior, even though she thought she was trying her hardest. Her tri-weekly runs through the farmland and the forest trails suddenly seemed to be inadequate in terms of fitness building.

She, too, should be heading to a gym in the early morning to lift enormous weights. The only problem was that the closest local gym was a twenty minute drive from her rural cottage, whereas the trails were a one-minute walk away. And it was lovely to run the route and listen to the sounds of nature.

May told herself she was not going to feel inferior. She was not. They were just different. And she needed to try take charge of this conversation.

"That sounds great, sis. So why are you calling?" May asked, tipping back her cup and taking a huge gulp of coffee.

Now that she'd updated her sister on her busy and important day, Kerry finally got around to the reason for her call.

"Yes. I just did the research on your suspect."

May felt a flare of excitement. This was sooner than she'd expected. Clearly intrigued, Kerry had made the time, and she couldn't be more grateful.

"Did you find anything out?" she asked eagerly. Surely her sister must have found something, to be calling so early.

"Well, to cut to the chase, I think you're wrong about your guess." Kerry sounded exacting and professional. "I think your guy is pretty legit. You must have done something incorrectly in the search."

May felt a rush of disappointment.

"Really? Are you sure?" she asked forlornly.

She'd been certain that she'd been correct. And if Kerry said he was legit, that really didn't bode well. Where had they managed to miss the information, she wondered, feeling small all over again.

Then Kerry let out a splutter of laughter.

"I'm kidding you, sis. You were absolutely right. In fact, I'm super impressed that you looked back so far. I carried on the research on my side, and I must say, he was hard to find."

"He was?" May asked, feeling a surprising head rush at her sister's praise.

"I ended up using facial recognition software from the pics you sent, combined with a few other classified tools and programs we have available. And eventually I worked out who he was."

"Who was he?"

"Your Coach Adamson used to be known as Walter Deeney. That's his birth name. He lived in Minneapolis most of his life and he taught P.E. But then, he got arrested and he ended up doing six months' jail time."

"What was the arrest for?" May's heart was beating faster now, and not just because of the double strength coffee.

"For statutory rape. Which means, of course, he had an affair with an underage girl. I'm guessing he couldn't keep his hands off his students."

"What?" Now May practically choked on her brew.

"He obviously decided to make a fresh start and take on a new name. And he must have guessed that at a small country school they wouldn't do the correct reference checks. Which I guess they didn't, at any rate, not at the first one where I see he worked before moving to the high school four years ago. Clearly, people didn't bother, and it never got picked up."

Kerry sounded annoyed by small town people who didn't do their job properly.

"So he changed his name and basically started again," May said, feeling stunned.

"Yep. And this time, his new name has no record of sexual misconduct associated with it."

May took a deep breath. She felt almost a bit dizzy.

"Thank you so much, Kerry, you're a superstar. This is such important news. I feel this is going to take us a lot further on the case."

"You're welcome, sis. I'm glad I could help."

It was all too much for her to take in at once. But May was feeling excited that she had been correct, and that they now had an extremely strong new suspect.

"Right, I have to go and jump in the shower. We're about to board the copter. You be careful out there."

"Thanks, Kerry, I appreciate all your help."

"Catch him, May. Go get him. I'll be thinking of you this morning."

"I owe you big time."

"You owe me nothing," Kerry said kindly. "Except a few wedding venue visits, of course, once Mom's done the first pass of venue research. And also most likely, some help with the flowers, and some of the work on getting the catering organized. And there are a few pre- and post-wedding events that I have in mind where I'll definitely need your organizational expertise with invites, timing, menus and so on."

"No problem," May said, realizing that she was completely over a barrel on this one and could absolutely not argue back.

"Apart from that, you owe me nothing. We're family, right? We look out for each other."

"We do," May said, feeling strangely touched, even though the list of responsibilities Kerry had in mind for her was extremely concerning and seemed to be lengthening by the moment.

"Good luck."

Kerry cut the call.

May downed the last of her coffee and rushed back to her bedroom.

This theory of hers had gotten the most surprising results. She'd never thought that Coach Adamson would have an actual arrest record.

Furthermore, it was for illegal activities with teenage girls which linked strongly to the current crimes.

The man was clearly the worst kind of predator and now, May suspected, he'd taken his urges to the next level. No longer was he having affairs with students. Instead, he was murdering his targets. May had never known that such behavior could escalate in that way. But she was about to confirm whether it had.

It was time to head out and go straight to pick up Coach Adamson for questioning.

CHAPTER EIGHTEEN

The teacher was a cunning planner. He thought ahead every step of the way. And now, his clever thinking was about to bear fruit.

Three victims.

He thought of them as his own personal second princess, first princess, and the queen. And now, the plan was in motion.

He'd been in the background at the start, and now, he was taking center stage once again. He'd sacrificed the second princess and the first princess. But now, his ultimate prize awaited, the one he had longed for the most.

His queen. His beautiful queen. His pulse quickened as he neared her house.

He'd been able to watch her movements so carefully in order to devise the perfect strategy, the moment when he took her.

He'd never done anything like this before. It was so exciting.

A lifetime of ordinary, humdrum activity had now culminated in this moment. He'd always known he was special, and had the ability to do things differently. He'd been dreaming of this for many long years until he'd put it to the test.

And now, the moment was here.

He could feel her fate close in.

Because of circumstances, he knew that this time would have to be different. It couldn't be the same as the others. Circumstances, after all, were different now. There was a sense of fear in the community.

Being able to take her at all was a massive achievement that had required cunning and skill. Even he had been surprised by his own talents in that direction.

But he wanted to take his time with her. He wasn't going to rush it. He needed to take her now, because it was his only chance. But last night, he'd had a message about an emergency staff meeting in the morning that had thrown his plans out.

So, he had decided to wait until school was out, and then spend the afternoon with her. He wanted to go slow. She was, after all, his queen.

He'd taken the others quickly and there had been great satisfaction in that, but he hadn't had time to speak with them. To share his feelings. To let them know how he truly felt about their beauty.

And then, to linger over ending her life to create the perfect experience, one he would look back on forever, feeling all the more delight and glee that his actions had never been discovered.

She'll be so surprised when she sees me, he thought.

And then he imagined her gasping for breath, as he squeezed the last of the breath out of her body.

He could see her, now, in his mind's eye. He closed his eyes, to indulge in the vision.

He smiled as he imagined her, the queen he'd been wanting to claim so badly.

Now, as her house came into view, he could feel his heart pounding with excitement. The teacher looked at the house. She was in there. The best part of him was in there. She was a perfect reflection of him. And soon, they would be together.

He waited. He knew it wouldn't take long.

Sure enough, a few minutes later, he saw the flicker of movement at her window that he'd been expecting.

He had a good feeling about this. His plans were going to be successful. The girl had no way of knowing that he was about to make his move. It would be seamless.

He wasn't nervous. He had everything worked out perfectly. He just wished he'd had more time to enjoy the moment.

Even though he knew he would be excited and full of tension, he'd need to appear calm.

There she was. He felt his heart pound as he saw her let herself out of the front door and head down the street.

It was light, and the sun was just up. She was walking fast in the morning's chill, with her gym bag slung over her shoulder, because this beautiful queen liked to go to the gym before school started on Mondays. He had to time this perfectly. Not too soon, that would be suspicious. But not too late, or there would be no point to it.

He had to wait for the right moment. There were already people on the street, in the distance. Far enough away for them not to be able to identify him. But he couldn't risk them coming any closer.

Wait, the teacher told himself. Wait, wait, be calm.

Now!

Smoothly, he drove forward, taking an earlier turn to join up with the main road, so it would look like he was just driving down it coincidentally.

There she was, his shy queen. Walking fast, her head bowed. So beautiful and she didn't even know it.

He drove up alongside her. She was so lovely. His heart was beating fast. This was it. This was the moment he'd been waiting for.

She glanced to the side as she saw his car. Her eyes widened in recognition. She saw him. She knew him.

He buzzed down his window.

"Good morning, Berenice," he said, savoring her name.

"Morning, sir," she said with a quick smile.

"You want a ride?" he offered. "I'm a little concerned to see you walking to school so early, especially after what's happened. It might not be safe."

She grimaced. "Yeah. I know. I was feeling anxious out here. Thanks. I'd love a ride."

She sounded relieved. He was glad of that. He wanted her to be comfortable with him.

He was glad she was smiling. She was so beautiful. He simply couldn't wait for the scenario ahead. He couldn't wait for the time when she would be his.

"Hop in," he said.

She opened the passenger door and slipped in, sitting down beside him.

He pulled out slowly, so as not to arouse suspicion. As if he was an ordinary person just helping out one of his students.

"How are you?" he asked her, casually, as he pulled back out into the street.

She shrugged. "Doing okay, I guess."

"I'm sorry you're having to go through all this," he said. "It's really been hard for everyone at the school."

"I hope the police solve it soon. I really appreciate the ride," she said.

He smiled again. He glanced at her, as he continued to drive. She was so pretty. She was his most valuable prize. And now, at last, he had her.

Discreetly, he pressed the central locking.

The other doors in the car all had child locks on them. That was part of his planning, and it had been so easy to do.

She was captured now. She was his.

He would need to gag her, tie her, and leave her somewhere where only he would know to come back to. He knew the forest trails well, and knew which ones were never used.

He had the perfect place in mind where he was certain she would not be found.

There were even flowers nearby. He'd noticed them yesterday. Beautiful flowers, in shades of pink and purple.

He would take her to the place he planned, and she would wait there for him. It would make the process even more exciting. Nobody would find her and she would not escape. He would attend the meeting and then he would return to her.

Waiting longer would only make the experience more pleasant.

At the point where he should have driven to the school, he flattened his foot on the gas and took the other route, speeding away, ignoring her frightened cry, because she was his now.

She was his victim. She was his queen.

His plan was working perfectly.

He'd captured his final prize, and now, he would take her somewhere, where she could wait for him. The future was ahead. He had everything planned out. He wanted to savor this last moment of having this beautiful girl in his possession.

This was going to be his ultimate sacrifice, the experience he would cherish forever.

CHAPTER NINETEEN

May headed out of the house, her tiredness forgotten, adrenaline spiking because she could well be on her way to the killer.

Automatically, she reached for the phone to call Owen as she climbed into the car.

And then she hesitated.

She wasn't sure that would be the best decision after what had happened between them last night. She felt this needed more time to settle.

But then May told herself not to be ridiculous. Of course Owen needed to be there. She couldn't let the personal predicament between them affect the way she did her job. Lives were at stake! This was no time to be a wilting flower because of what had happened yesterday. She'd just have to toughen up and set her emotions aside.

Taking a deep breath, she dialed his number.

"Hello?" he answered on the second ring, sounding snappish. Her stomach plummeted. It was as if he was a stranger.

"I got information on Coach Adamson from Kerry, and it's not looking good for him," May said. "He has been operating under a false name, and has a record of statutory rape."

Owen gasped.

"We need to go and speak to him as soon as we can. He lives in Floral Ridge."

"I'll be there. But it won't be soon. I wasn't home last night. I was on the other side of the lake."

It really was just like talking to a stranger. She felt terrible. Had he gone to a friend for company? What had happened last night? Normally he'd tell her, but not this time.

"I'll give you the address," she said. "You can meet me there, and I'll call in some other backup so we don't waste time."

"Alright." He cut the call abruptly as soon as she'd read out the address.

With an effort, May put the emotional entanglement of this situation firmly out of her mind. There wasn't time for it right now. On the trail of a suspect, every moment counted.

With Owen delayed, May decided to call the local police department in Floral Ridge.

She got on the phone again immediately.

"I'm on my way to pick up a suspect in a murder investigation, and I need some help," she said. "The suspect's name is Graeme Adamson, and he resides at number 4 Boardwalk Street. Could someone meet me there in fifteen minutes?"

"Sure, we'll be there," the local cop said.

At this early hour, there was no sign of the Monday morning traffic that May knew would clutter up the roads within the next hour or so. Right now her headlights cut the gloom as she sped along almost empty roads. She didn't bother with the sirens, just drove as fast as she could.

Her mind was focused on the takedown ahead.

As she drove the car down the country lanes, May realized she felt totally awake and buzzing with adrenaline. Not surprising, seeing as she was going after a villain who was wanted for multiple crimes, who was a dangerous threat to the community, and who would hopefully soon be locked away in a maximum-security prison.

She was feeling shivery and excited at the thought of it. Her senses were heightened and she was feeling a sense of exhilaration, and also of relief, that their lakeside towns would soon be safe from the man terrorizing them.

As May turned onto Boardwalk Street in the quiet town of Floral Ridge, she saw a police car parked by the side of the road ahead, under a maple tree. An older police officer, who she recognized, climbed out.

"Morning, Deputy Moore. Congratulations on your promotion – last month, was it? You deserve it."

"Morning, Deputy Edwards, and thank you," she replied, glad to have his experience and skill in what might prove to be a violent confrontation.

"I have two more officers coming as backup," Deputy Edwards said, looking at his watch. "They should be here any moment."

"Thanks," May said, feeling relief. "Shall we make a start?"

He nodded. "Let's do that."

May got out of the car and headed over to the front door of the house. Edwards kept pace with her as she headed up the neatly paved path, past the mowed front yard. Everything was trim and tidy. This didn't seem like the home where a criminal fugitive had been hiding. He had kept his secrets well, May thought. He'd clearly presented a very different, and respectable, front to the world.

Swallowing hard, she knocked on the door.

Then she and Edwards waited expectantly.

In her mind, May recalled the features of the man who would open it any moment. Coach Adamson was six foot tall, according to the information. He had a strong face, chestnut hair, and blue eyes. He looked every inch the respectable P.E. coach, and she was sure that his good, clean-cut looks and handsome features had counted in his favor.

But why wasn't he coming to the door?

May sensed movement behind her and glanced around, but it was just the backup police car pulling up outside the house. Two officers climbed out and headed up the path to stand behind them.

Across the road, May saw a woman in a dressing gown peering curiously out of her front door. From the main road, a couple of blocks away, the hum of Monday morning traffic was getting louder.

She knocked again.

"He might already have left," the policeman muttered.

The woman in the dressing gown crossed the road.

"If you're looking for Mr. Adamson, he's already left," she called. "I saw him leave here about half an hour ago. He drove that way." She pointed west.

Seemingly satisfied at having helped the police, she turned and padded back, in her pink slippers, across the road again.

"Always good to have informative neighbors," Edwards acknowledged. "It's early on a Monday. Would he have gone to the gym?"

"More likely, he headed straight to the school," May said. "It's a few miles away in that direction, and there's a gym there, I'm sure. I think we should go there immediately. But let's leave someone here at his house, in case he comes back. We don't want him being tipped off that we were here, and destroying any evidence."

Edwards nodded. "Good thinking. Officer Emerson, please stay here. If you see the suspect, call for backup and make an immediate arrest."

With all bases covered, May hoped, she climbed into the car and set off on the short drive to Sleepy Hollow School.

The sense of anticipation was building as she sped along the road, and she felt her body tense as she got ready for action. Arriving at the school, she parked at the far end of the parking lot and waited for the other police car to pull up.

The school, in the town of Sleepy Hollow which neighbored Floral Ridge, was a small high school that catered to around three hundred students. It was set in a large building that was an old converted hotel, with a charming colonial-style frontage.

May felt a weird sense of dislocation as she climbed out of the car, knowing she would be entering this scenic building on the chase for a criminal.

She caught her breath as she saw the flower arrangements placed outside the building. There were three parents standing in silence, holding protest notices.

"Save Our Students, Keep them Home," one read. "Keep Our Schools Safe," another read.

"What are you doing to stop these crimes, officers?" one of the parents called angrily as the police trooped upstairs and headed inside. "I'm not sending my girls back to school until I know this is under control!"

"Are you attending the school staff meeting? The principal just told us he's holding an emergency meeting at eight," another parent shouted.

"We're actively investigating and that's why we are here, following a suspect," May said breathlessly. "I hope we will make an arrest very soon."

So there was a staff meeting at eight? Clearly the school was calling in the staff to discuss their strategy for the safety of the students. May hoped that if things went the way she intended, by the time the meeting was over, they wouldn't have to worry anymore.

Then, with no more time to spare, she rushed ahead.

There was the school staff room. She veered right and headed for the open door. Already, at this early hour, there were two teachers inside.

They both turned, looking curious and apprehensive, as the police arrived at the door.

"Can we help you?" the older teacher, a gray-haired woman, asked.

"Coach Adamson. Where can we find him?"

"He's in the gym, I believe," the older teacher said, but as May was about to turn away, the other teacher shook his head.

"I saw him heading out to the football field. He's doing an early coaching session with the team. With this emergency staff meeting ahead, it had to take place earlier than usual," he said gravely.

"Thank you," May said.

They hustled out of the staff room and rushed through the school corridors, out of the far entrance to the brilliant green playing fields beyond.

She saw him in the distance. He was standing on the grass, talking to a group of players, who were gathered around. The tall coach had a whistle around his neck, and was holding a clipboard in his hand.

May hurried across the grass as fast as she could.

Even from a distance, she could see he was a physically powerful man, and she felt tense with apprehension. This was it, she thought, the moment of truth when they would confront Adamson and make their move.

He spotted her as she neared him, and his shoulders stiffened with shock. She saw his face harden with fear and anger, as he realized she meant business.

"What are you doing here?" he asked.

"We need to question you regarding the recent murders," May said firmly.

"This is madness!" Adamson exclaimed. "You're making a huge mistake. I have nothing to do with those murders. And you're disrupting important coaching time. I thought the police was supposed to be here to help the community."

There was a sneering tone in his voice that got May's back right up.

"Don't make this difficult for yourself," May warned. "We know who you are. We know you've been living under an assumed name for the last eight years, and that you have previous convictions attached to your real name, Walter Deeney."

Now, his face contorted with rage and fear.

She took a step toward him, but to her shock, he suddenly swung a punch at her. She ducked instinctively, astonished, but the punch caught her shoulder and she staggered back.

And then, Coach Adamson, aka Walter Deeney, flung his clipboard at her, turned and began sprinting in the other direction, cutting through the scattering of students on the bleachers, knocking one right off his feet in his haste to get away.

The clipboard hit her in the elbow. Luckily she'd gotten her hand up in time, or it would have hit her in the face.

"Quick! Chase him!"

Striding as fast as she could, May set off in pursuit.

This man was guilty, without a doubt. He'd just tried to assault her. She'd seen the murderous rage in his eyes. Now, she was going to chase after him, and be ready for whatever he might try to do to save himself.

CHAPTER TWENTY

May set off in pursuit of the fleeing coach, with the police officers flanking her. Together, they scrambled up the bleachers to the walkway at the top. As May charged along, her phone began ringing loudly.

She grabbed it out of her pocket and saw it was Owen.

Knowing that it would slow her down, but needing to speak to her deputy, she grabbed the call.

"I'm at the house! There's one other officer here. Where are you?" he snapped.

"I'm chasing Adamson down at the school, with the Floral Ridge officers," she shouted breathlessly.

"Should I join you?"

May considered that question as she plowed along, losing ground behind the other three men.

"Yes, join me."

May shoved the phone back in her pocket and increased her speed again. Her lungs were burning and she was gasping for air.

But she was not going to give up on this. She was determined to catch him.

The others were outstripping her, but she gave it her all, tearing after them as they disappeared into the distance.

She saw Coach Adamson ahead of her, weaving through the corner of the building and around to the left, through a group of parents clustered in the back parking lot, who parted quickly as he barreled straight through them.

"Stop! Police!" May called out, hoping to scare him into slowing down, but he didn't stop. He sprinted past the parents, who stared at him in shock.

"What do you think you're doing?" one of the women yelled angrily after him.

But Adamson just increased his speed, and now his lead was even greater. There was no way that they were going to outrun a tall, fit man who spent all day coaching football players, May realized with a thud of her stomach.

That meant she had to try and find another way to catch up.

May narrowed her eyes. Thinking logically, Adamson had not escaped the school grounds. Therefore, there was only one place he could go along the route he was taking. And that was into the school building.

He was going to head inside, and that made her nervous. This violent, desperate man could do anything at this stage. He could take a hostage. He could assault somebody else. He could pull out a gun and start shooting.

The possibilities were scary.

But if she went in the near side of the school building, then she'd be able to come face to face with him as he blasted his way through. Rather than tagging along getting further and further behind the others, she needed to think on her feet and get ahead.

Work smart, not hard, as she was sure Kerry would have quipped. Although, Kerry would probably have grabbed his arm when he threw that punch and arrested him there and then.

Her mind made up, May peeled off the path, hurtling toward the main school building. The plan was to head inside and try and catch up with him from the opposite direction to make the arrest. If he made any move to hurt anybody, May knew she would have to be ready.

It felt cool and dark inside, after the bright morning sunlight outside.

She glanced around, trying to calm her breath. She was relieved to see that there were no students in the corridors. She was sure that a lot of students had stayed home today.

But where was Adamson? She needed to hustle through to the other side of the building, because that was where he would come in, or at least, so she hoped.

Sticking to the walls, May stayed in the shadows, moving swiftly towards the end of the corridor, where there was a stairwell.

From ahead, she heard pounding footsteps and shouting, and knew he was on the run and heading inside, just as she thought he would do. This was her chance to come face to face with him, and next time, if he tried another punch, she'd be ready for him. Preferably, with her weapon aimed at him, May resolved.

Then, as she reached the corner and edged around it, she heard a commotion. Adamson was there, ahead of her, running toward her, but as soon as he saw her, he veered to the right, racing up the stairwell.

Feeling encouraged that she was now close behind him, May followed him. She pounded up the steps two or three at a time, trying to keep up with the man in front of her.

Then, with a shout, he sprinted through the archway, and onto the gallery at the top of the stairs.

She dashed up to the gallery, following him.

"Police!" she shouted. "Stop where you are!"

She saw Adamson turn and look behind him, and she saw his eyes widen in fear as he saw her.

With a cry of desperation, he shoved aside one student who was walking toward the stairs. Shouting in surprise, the young man sprawled backward against the railing.

Adamson ran for the double doors at the end of the gallery.

He swerved to the left, darting across the arched corridor and into the library.

"No! Don't you dare go in there!" May shouted, powering after him, terrified once again that someone would end up in a hostage situation.

The librarian was at her desk. At the sound of running footsteps, she leapt to her feet, her mouth opening in a cry of protest, but it was too late.

"Stay out of this, please, ma'am. This could be dangerous," May yelled as she raced in.

The librarian ducked down, looking horrified and afraid as May chased Adamson through the quiet, carpeted room.

There were a couple of people reading, but they all looked up, then ducked their heads down again when they realized what was happening.

Adamson ran through the library, knocking over chairs and weaving between the desks. With an athletic leap, he jumped straight over a desk, knocking over a laptop computer, which clattered on the floor.

Darting around the desk, May followed in hot pursuit.

There was a fire door at the back which he wrenched open. Hurtling out, he raced down the corridor, past two closed doors. He pulled open the third door and bolted inside.

Who was there? Were they safe?

Anxiety flared in May as she pounded along the corridor and, with her head down, sprinted for the door, hoping she would reach it before he had the chance to slam it in her face. She tried to keep calm, even though she was very aware that Adamson was a desperate man.

She skidded to a stop as she reached it, and barged her shoulder into the partly closed door, seeing at the last moment that there was a sign on it: *Coach Adamson: Private Office.*

May skidded inside, gasping, taking in the room.

It was a small room, with a sunny window at the back.

There was a desk with two chairs and a computer, a small sofa, and a large filing cabinet.

Coach Adamson was standing on the far side of the room, near the open cabinet.

He had a wild expression in his blue eyes, and a gun in his hand.

CHAPTER TWENTY ONE

May's heart jumped all the way into her throat as she saw the long barrel and black muzzle of that gun, gripped tightly in Coach Adamson's hand.

But it wasn't aimed at her.

The muscular coach had the gun pointed at his own head, his finger tight on the trigger.

There wasn't time for her to draw her own weapon. In the mad chase to catch up with him she hadn't grabbed it out of the holster. Now she couldn't. Moving her hand toward the grip of her gun would be an extremely unwise move. Because he was watching her hand. And her gun.

She knew she had to defuse the situation, but that was easier said than done. She stopped just inside the door, and even though she was gasping from the chase, she tried to slow her movements right down, making no sudden motion with her hands or arms.

"Coach Adamson, no," she said, keeping her voice steady and calm, even though she wanted to be sick with fear. "Please, don't do anything reckless now."

She couldn't face the thought of having him shoot himself in front of her. It would be extremely traumatic, not only for her, but for the whole school and the community.

"I need to be free of this guilt," he said, staring at her. He sounded confused, almost in shock.

"We can talk about that in a minute," May said calmly. "For now, please, put the gun down."

"You don't understand," he said. "I have to be free. I don't want to live anymore! I don't want to be a monster!"

"Don't do anything you'll regret!" May emphasized to him.

She knew that it was always a risk when approaching a man with a gun. He could change his mind at any second and pull the trigger, before she had time to make the arrest. They still needed a confession from him, and to find out more information. He was only a suspect, and the guilt he was feeling might be from his past. There were many rational reasons why it was imperative for them to bring him in.

"I didn't mean to do it. It was like I couldn't help myself," he stammered.

"I'd like to hear more about that. We definitely need to talk about it. To discuss it," May said, talking even more calmly.

She had to try and keep him talking, to keep him focused, to get him off the precipice of tension where he was wobbling.

"Put the gun down, Coach Adamson. You can get the help you need," she urged.

A tear fell down the man's cheek.

"I'm so sorry," he said, his voice cracking. "I didn't mean for any of it to happen."

He was sweating heavily and his skin looked pale, almost as if he had been ill for some time. His outdoor tan had all but disappeared, drowned in the terrified pallor.

"Please, put the gun down," May said, fighting to hold her voice steady.

"I can't change what I did," he protested. "I can't change the past."

"None of us are able to do that," May said, trying to sound soothing, even though she didn't feel it inside. She thought that the guy was a violent bully and that he had serious blood on his hands. "You can get help. You don't have to do this."

"I have ruined my life. I have ruined so many other lives," he said, staring at the gun as if it represented his only remaining solution.

"Shooting yourself now is not the answer. We need to talk this through together now," May argued. She wanted to question him. She needed to know what had caused this man to go on a killing spree.

"But my life is over anyway. There's no way I can go on," he said, taking a step toward her. Her eyes narrowed as she saw his finger tighten.

"Maybe I should shoot you. Maybe I should shoot everyone. There's no point anymore."

May's eyes widened.

He was unpredictable, driven now by pure fear. May knew that he might shoot himself, but in his overwrought state, he could just as easily decide to turn the gun her way. In fact, with a shaking hand, he was doing just that, and now she was staring straight into the barrel.

"Don't do anything that you'll regret," she said again. Gathering all her courage, she stepped forward. "You really don't want to shoot me," she said kindly. "It would hurt a lot, and I would start yelling, and it would make a terrible mess in your office."

"I guess it would," he said, distracted by that thought.

"And you'd only end up in more trouble," May pushed. "All we need to do now is talk about this and find out the facts."

"Why do you keep saying I'll regret this?" he asked, agonized. "It's a sensible decision. My only one so far."

"Please!" she repeated, trying not to sound too forceful or too threatening. "Just set the gun down and we can talk about this."

Looking uncertain, he turned the barrel to face the wall. Now it was pointing at neither of them, and that was a huge improvement.

With a flash of relief May heard the clatter of footsteps behind her. The other officers had arrived.

Edwards and one of the other officers burst in the door and to May's utter relief, they had their guns drawn and were ready for him.

"Put the gun down, sir. Lower your weapon immediately," Edwards called out in a steady but commanding voice.

Their arrival gave Coach Adamson a shock. He glanced from one to the other, looking confused, and then hastily lowered his weapon.

May felt a massive surge of relief. Her heart dropped back down to its normal place in her chest.

Edwards quickly moved forward and removed the gun from Adamson's hand, while May got out the handcuffs. Never had she heard such a welcome sound as when they clamped shut around his wrists. That stand-off had been terrifying.

"Thank you," she said to her colleagues, her voice hoarse. She looked at the coach, who was staring at them with a bewildered expression.

"I didn't want it to happen," he said, staring at his hands. "It just happened," he repeated.

"You can lower your weapons now," Edwards said, to his two colleagues. Then turning back to Adamson, he continued. "That's all for now, sir. The deputy will take it from here. You come along with us."

"I guess I'm finished," he said, sounding completely lost.

May reached over and took the gun from the floor, keeping her eyes fixed on its owner.

"You really need to tell us everything you can. We need to make sense of it all."

She hoped that she would be able to get a full confession out of him. Because this man, under his former grinning, tanned facade, was nothing more than an evil monster.

As the police were escorting Coach Adamson downstairs, May's phone rang again.

It was Owen.

"I just got here," he said. "Are you okay?"

He still sounded grumpy, but not as much like a stranger as he had.

"I'm okay. We've just arrested him," she said.

She hoped that they might be able to uncover more evidence that would allow them to put this case to rest for good. Adamson had kept a gun in his office filing cabinet on school premises, which was a felony, but it was not related to strangling young women to death. There was still a lot that she needed to prove regarding these crimes.

Suddenly, May had an idea.

"Owen, I'm going to have a quick look around his office. And while we're both here, let's seize his keys and search his car. There could be evidence there. Trace evidence, or some other links that might help to tie him to the crimes."

May felt hopeful about the car.

Getting into Coach Adamson's mind, she thought that if she had been him, that was where she would have kept her secrets. Close by and easily accessible, suiting his obsessive, criminal nature.

CHAPTER TWENTY TWO

May began a thorough search of Coach Adamson's office, carefully opening each drawer in that big filing cabinet, and looking in his desk drawers. She was hopeful to find any shred of evidence.

But to her disappointment, the filing cabinet didn't hold a treasure trove of papers it was a depository for sporting equipment. Old footballs, shin guards, baseball caps, and a few lighter dumbbells. The gun must have been in there, which May thought was unusual, but there was nothing else noteworthy to be seen.

How about the desk?

Here, too, she was disappointed. Only a few pens and pencils, a blank notepad, an old calculator, and a few till slips for sporting items were there. There was no sign of any untoward communication with students, and not even so much as a wilted rose petal to link him with the bodies.

Sighing, May left the office, locking it behind her, and headed downstairs. She walked down the corridor, where knots of students were staring curiously at her.

The school environment felt unfamiliar to her. It had been a long time since she'd been in a school.

She had never been a rebellious student and had spent most of her time buried in her books, encouraged by her mother to do better than Kerry and better than Lauren.

"I want you to beat your sisters and get the best grades of all," Mrs. Moore had harangued her.

Of course, she'd told Kerry and Lauren exactly the same thing, with the result that the sisters were endlessly pitted against each other in a competitive environment by their perfectionist, ex-schoolteacher mother.

No wonder they'd ended up with issues, May thought sadly.

She guessed even Kerry, the golden child and highest achiever, had suffered. Kerry didn't need to feel jealous, ever. But May had been stunned to realize that, sometimes, she did.

All the teachers were inside the staff room now. May guessed the meeting was in full swing, discussing and strategizing. The thought of what they were going through made her feel really bad that they had not yet concluded the case. It motivated her to work her hardest. This needed resolution. These teachers did not deserve this.

As she walked past the small groups of students, May heard whispers, and conversations in hushed voices.

Everyone knew something was up. Many of them must have seen Coach Adamson being taken away by the police. But, as she passed the students, she also picked up that they sounded confused and defensive of their coach.

She guessed that was to be expected. A predator might only focus his attentions on a chosen few, while the others thought he was a blameless and wonderful teacher. But May knew already that it would make their job harder. Some people might speak in favor of Adamson's character, and that meant the chain of evidence, and the testimony from the coach himself, would be even more important.

With any luck, May hoped, she would have a full confession by the time the meeting concluded, but any additional testimony would back it up.

Crime caused such ripples throughout a community. In a small town, she always felt that she, as a policewoman, experienced them more intensely.

Coach Adamson had definitely seemed like a broken man. He'd been at rock bottom, ready to end his life - or at any rate, threatening to. The way she handled this questioning would be vital. They needed to know more about his movements during the night of the prom. She needed to get into his mind and find out why and how he'd done these things.

Why the strangulation?

Why the flowers?

She didn't recall him giving any concrete facts. He'd been a fountain of self blame but no actual information had come out of his mouth during his diatribe.

They would need a lot more than what he'd given so far to secure a conviction.

She hoped that without the confession, their case would be close to watertight. But if they could get a confession, they could truly wipe this case clean.

However, May was concerned that his planning was so meticulous that he could have thought ahead to implement a defense or an alibi somehow. A well-planned defense could always sway the jury.

"I'm going to kill myself," he'd said, but that was hardly evidence, she thought, feeling frustrated.

Plus, some people had what May thought of as rubber feet. They might hit rock bottom but they could bounce back from it at surprising speed.

May was sure that many people close to the coach would want to believe that he was innocent. Strong, good looking P.E. coaches were influential figures and people looked up to them.

And if there were still a lot of people who believed that he was a hero, despite all the evidence to the contrary, then she would have to work hard to get the evidence to prove his guilt.

At least when they'd confronted him that morning, he'd committed minor crimes in front of witnesses, which even though it had been scary at the time, May felt very glad about. They had needed that.

Coach Adamson had remained in hiding from his previous identity for eight years. If it hadn't been for May's observant nature and Kerry's FBI access, they would still not know who he had been. He was a master at covering his tracks and putting on a convincing front.

They needed more!

If they could get a full confession, they would be able to hold him accountable.

May bit her lip as she walked to the school entrance, wishing that they had something to push him in that direction, either to use as evidence or else to pressure the coach in another way.

And at that moment, she heard Owen calling to her loudly from the staff parking lot.

He was standing by an ordinary looking car, similar to a lot of others that the teachers seemed to drive.

"May! Come quick! I think I've seen something here!" he shouted.

May rushed out of the school entrance, racing to the parking lot on legs that felt surprisingly tired after the adrenaline-fueled pursuit earlier. But now, determination gave her feet fresh wings.

"What is it?" she called to Owen.

She didn't know what Owen had seen, but if it was anything to do with Coach Adamson's guilt, then she was all ears. Plus, he was sounding more and more like himself again and she felt a flash of relief that they might be able to get back to being friends.

"This is Coach Adamson's car," he called back. "I have confirmed it with the staff office. I haven't searched inside yet, but it looks to be unlocked, so we might not need the key. Anyway I peered through the window and this is weird, May! Weird!"

101

"What is it?"

May hurried closer.

Owen was bent over the passenger window, gazing through the lightly tinted glass.

"Can you see anything?" she asked.

"Have a look," he said.

May bent over and gazed along with him.

She drew in a gasp.

"Those? What are they?"

Immediately, she saw a face she recognized on a printed page. Sadie's face was staring out from it.

May's mouth felt dry. She couldn't believe it. Right here, right now, it seemed they had the evidence they needed.

CHAPTER TWENTY THREE

May couldn't believe that at this critical time, they might possibly have found something that could make this case watertight. Her heart was pounding with excitement as she quickly pulled on the gloves that Owen was handing to her, and scraped her hair back, trapping it under a head cover. If Adamson had been careless about leaving things in his car, that also meant the car could be a treasure trove of trace evidence. It would need to be forensically examined, but for now, May didn't want to delay the initial search.

She grabbed the car door and yanked it open.

There, on the passenger seat, was a folder labeled "Athletic Reports."

So innocent looking, if it had not been for that corner of a page jutting out, and Sadie's distinctive photo being visible.

"Son of a gun," May muttered.

She grabbed the folder and opened it up, her heart thumping with excitement. This was not a folder of athletic reports.

Owen hissed in a breath.

"What was he up to?" he whispered incredulously.

She saw at least a dozen photos of Sadie, printed out in full, glossy color. Each one must have been snapped by Coach Adamson, at different moments during the school day.

May glanced at the photos, feeling horrified and angry.

The first photo showed Sadie on the steps at school, talking to a group of friends. They were all laughing. In the next one that he'd taken, she was standing by her locker, chatting to another friend. In the next one, out on the track, she was jogging and smiling.

In the next one, she was walking from her car to the school entrance.

"He had her practically under surveillance," May murmured. "She didn't even know he was watching her!"

"He's been spying on her. This is seriously strong evidence. He'll go down for this," Owen said with a tight voice. "This is just proof that he's been stalking Sadie all over town. Any jury would take one look at this and nail him. Nail him good."

May flipped back through the folder.

There were pictures of Alyssa. Her heart clenched as she saw the pretty girl in her cheerleader outfit, still smiling, still unaware that her life was in danger. Smiling at a point to the right of the camera, she was seemingly unaware that she was being photographed.

May peered closely at the photo. "He was watching her all the time. That's how he gets away with it. He knows them, and he's charming."

"This is creepy," Owen said. "She looks so happy. This is a school day, and he's watching her and taking these pics. At school! As a teacher."

May let out a slow breath, her anger rising.

"I'll call this in." May was almost relieved that they had the evidence, now. There was still a lot of work to do, but at least now, they were heading in the right direction.

"He clearly recorded everything about them," Owen said. "He must have been obsessed with them."

"That's what it takes," May said. "And at least now, we have some proof. This is the evidence we need to ensure that he is never going to hurt another girl again."

She looked at the photos and shivered at the thought of a man like the coach stalking innocent girls.

The coach was finished. He'd been caught and there was no way that he would escape this time. With this concrete evidence now providing the backbone of the case, May felt much more confident about the interview itself.

And she was glad that they weren't going to rely on a confession alone.

"Is there anything else we can use here?" she asked. This was exciting but it didn't mean they should give up.

"There's a laptop in the trunk. We can take that in. Hopefully he'll give us the sign-in code," Owen said.

Corroborating evidence on a laptop would be another huge win.

Her heart was beating faster, now that she saw what they had. They could finally nail him.

Perhaps, knowing that they were in possession of these photos might be enough to break him. May felt increasingly certain that this hard evidence would provide what was needed for Coach Adamson to crumble.

Now, they just had to go and confront him with it.

*

Fifteen minutes later, May and Owen pulled up outside the Floral Ridge police department where Adamson had been taken. May had waited at the school until the forensic detectives had arrived to begin their examination of the car. She didn't want to leave it unattended for a moment. She hoped that the car would provide some trace evidence. A smear of blood, a filament of the petals from the flowers he had left on the scene. Something that could link him to the crimes beyond any reasonable doubt.

There was a positive atmosphere at the police department. May sensed it as soon as she walked in. The officer at the desk beamed at her.

"Congratulations, Deputy Moore. I'm so relieved that this is concluded. You cannot believe how many calls we've had to field. Every parent in the entire Tamarack County has been in a state of panic."

"I can well believe it, and with good reason," May sympathized.

"It's so hard for us, as police, at the start of an investigation like this. I'm just thrilled that it hasn't dragged on."

"That's the worst situation," May agreed. "Panic turns sour and the police start to be blamed."

"And the public loses trust in us. It becomes such a toxic situation."

Worst case scenario it might be, but May knew that until the case had been finalized there was always the risk that they might catapult straight back into these dire circumstances.

"We are lucky that a good lead has taken us further," May acknowledged. "We have very strong proof that will back the case up, but it's not yet over. We want this case to be watertight. This next hour is going to be critically important."

Looking more somber now, the woman nodded.

"I need to remember that," she said. "I've seen many seemingly strong cases break on the rocks at the last moment. I sure hope this isn't one of them, although I know it's not always within your control."

"It happens," May agreed, feeling her mouth suddenly dry. This case could be one of them. She knew all too well that this happened. Witnesses could change their minds. Strong alibis could pop like rabbits out of a hat, causing surprise and despair and cracking a seemingly solid case apart.

She headed through to the interview room. Then she stood outside the door, preparing herself. She glanced at Owen, relieved in that moment that the awkwardness of earlier had vanished and it was just the two of them, on the fight for justice and looking to obtain the outcome they needed.

"I'll do the initial interview," May said firmly. "Will you start by checking his devices? We need proof from the phone and laptop, as soon as we can get it."

"Yes. I'll go do that. Good luck," Owen said, and hurried away.

May opened the door and walked in.

Coach Adamson stared up at her, hunched over the table.

He looked like a broken man, May thought. His handsome face was hollow with despair. His eyes blazed out, bright and frantic. His well manicured hands were clenched together on the wooden desk, so tightly enfolded that his tanned knuckles had gone white.

But as shattered as his demeanor looked, his words told a different story.

In a deep, shaking voice, he began to speak.

"I know why you brought me here. I didn't do it! I don't care what you think or how it looks. I didn't do it!" he pleaded, staring at May with forlorn hope in his eyes.

CHAPTER TWENTY FOUR

In the back office of the police precinct, Owen began working frantically. They needed evidence. Evidence, hard proof, to take this killer down.

In front of him he had the laptop from Coach Adamson's trunk, as well as his cellphone which had been taken from him when he had been checked into the police department.

Adamson had cooperated with police, giving them the access codes to both his devices.

Now, Owen had to check for any evidence that might be on these devices, either hidden away, or else in the record of messages, calls, or emails.

He pressed his lips together, aware of the seriousness of this task and also the pressure of time they were under. He'd watched the first few moments of the interview from the observation room, and it was clear that despite incriminating evidence in the form of the pictures, Coach Adamson was going to deny this every step of the way.

He would fight and fight as long as he could, employing every trick in the book. And then there was the fact he was a popular, respected figure in the community. That made it even more important that they dug up whatever evidence they could.

Owen did not have time to blink. He was fully alert, taking in every last detail, working with a steely determination. He had to find the evidence they needed.

As Owen scrolled to the places in both devices where he wanted to start, he found his thoughts going back to that disastrous conversation with May yesterday.

He could bang his head on the desk, thinking of how badly that had gone. He'd handled the whole thing appallingly. He'd chosen totally the wrong time. Congratulations, Owen, he told himself cynically.

He had rushed it, and then shyness had overwhelmed him, fear of rejection had loomed in his mind, and it had come out wrong.

She'd literally just misunderstood what he was saying. There had been issues with Dan's Bar, he'd realized that immediately. On the wrong foot from the start, he hadn't gotten the message across in any coherent way to sell the idea of going for a drink, to her. It had been disastrous.

Most humiliating of all, he was sure that somewhere along the line she'd realized what he meant. May was sharp; she'd just been distracted. His efforts had been too little, too late. She hadn't revisited the topic though, and now he had no idea where he stood with her.

But he had still had feelings there, feelings he needed to get out. He'd been thinking about May a lot as he'd driven to his brother's place, licking his wounds and in need of a few drinks. Even though he'd briefly thought she was insufferable, insensitive, and had broken his heart, deep down his mind had reminded him that she was the most amazing woman. Her integrity, her resolve, her compassion. Not to mention how he could drown in her bright blue eyes and felt warmed when she gave him that wickedly gorgeous smile.

He had barely been able to speak to her when she'd called the next morning. He'd felt offended, rejected, embarrassed, and as if he was suddenly a stranger to her. Thankfully, the events of the morning, happening so fast, had somehow smoothed things over.

Now, to his dismay, he was feeling a flare of hope again. He'd wanted that emotion gone forever, but here it was, back again.

Just a date. One date. Was it too much to ask for? Or should he give up on the idea and just feel grateful that they were in a comfortable and friendly relationship?

Which he hoped they could get back to after how badly last night had played out.

He felt embarrassed, unloved, rejected, and hurt. He also felt confused and angry with himself. But looking at another layer of his feelings, Owen found that he also felt determined that he was going to get things back on a workable footing.

May hadn't meant to hurt him. But now, the whole situation was difficult to talk about.

He closed his eyes for a moment, and then opened them again.

It was clear that what he needed to do now was focus. Thinking about May wouldn't help solve the crime. Not in any way. And mooning over her wouldn't impress her. Buckling down to work and finding critical evidence on these devices, however, would definitely impress her.

So, calls first.

Owen was relieved to see a record of the recent calls made to and from Adamson's cellphone. This was useful.

He scrolled through, looking at names, and keeping an eye out for any calls made to and from the recorded cellphone numbers of Sadie or Alyssa, both of which he had on file.

But as far as these records went back, Adamson hadn't spoken to either of them at all. He hadn't called them; they hadn't called him. He had made quite a few phone calls, but they had mostly been to football team members, his coaching colleagues, and a few personal calls to friends.

No Sadie, no Alyssa, although he guessed Adamson could have deleted such calls.

Their phone numbers had both been inputted into Adamson's contact list, though, Owen noted. He personally thought that was highly irregular, but he guessed that in today's digital age, Adamson would be able to defend himself by saying he'd done it so they could be in messaging groups and communicate more effectively.

And that was where he went next.

There, Owen realized, was a lot more to be picked up. Coach Adamson was a serial texter. There were reams of communications here. He had several groups set up on his phone to interact with students, and he had messaged both Sadie and Alyssa in the days before they died. He guessed that being in the special coaching group had provided a good excuse for that.

Owen quickly hunted through the messages, reading every last one.

The tone was definitely flirty. And the content was somewhat inappropriate. He called them 'angel' and 'sweetheart.' References were made to 'bikini ready bodies' that had Owen narrowing his eyes in anger. In a couple of the messages, he suggested one on one extra lessons, and that they should hook up with him for coffee.

That was definitely pointing to him wanting an inappropriate relationship. Owen thought, with a frustrated sigh, that he'd been allowed to get away with doing this. For sure, May could use this information. But as much as seeing these texts was disturbing, Owen was disappointed that there had been no direct solicitation of the girls. Also, he could see no fights or friction that could have pointed the way to a murder scenario erupting.

The girls seemed happy with his tone. They had replied with smiley emojis. And scrolling through other messages, Owen realized that Coach Adamson communicated this way very consistently. All the girls received the same warm, flirty, over-friendly treatment from this slimy man who had slept with one or more underage girls in the past.

His eyes opened wider as he saw messages to both girls saying, "See you at the prom! And the post-party!"

That was important, Owen thought, feeling as if he was now making progress. That was an important link in what was needed to nail this guy. He'd clearly shown that he intended to meet up with both his victims during that fateful night when Alyssa had been murdered. He could have been right on the scene, and grabbed the opportunity he was seeking.

But the investigator's side of Owen's brain was still needing more.

Emails? He turned to the laptop.

Scanning through, he saw there were a lot of emails in Adamson's inbox, too. Owen began scrolling through, noting that they were mostly from team members and colleagues. He clicked on the most recent, a few hours old.

It was from Coach White, a colleague, and it was a thank you note for all Adamson had done in the last few days.

He ran a search for Sadie's name, and then for Alyssa's. The girls came up here, too. In fact, they came up a lot. He frowned, going over the emails and reading them carefully.

There was nothing definitive here.

Most of them were feedback on assignments, progress reports as part of the coaching group, heads-up on televised events they might want to watch, and invitations to workshops and matches.

Nothing to indicate that Adamson was planning trouble or that there was a murderous rage just waiting to erupt.

Owen sighed in frustration. He was doing all he could. All they needed was some kind of evidence and they could nail this guy to the wall. But he was getting nowhere.

He glanced at his watch. He was doing nothing to help the timeline flow here.

Then Owen remembered there was one thing he could do. One thing that was going to be vitally important in linking the threads together.

The pictures.

He could create a timeline of when Coach Adamson had taken the shots, and see if that linked up to the messages. In fact, simply linking up the dates of those incriminating images with the communications, would be helpful.

Feeling that he might have the answers now, and hoping he'd be in time to help May, Owen went back to the coach's phone and quickly accessed the images.

CHAPTER TWENTY FIVE

May sat down opposite Coach Adamson, frowning at him sternly. She was not going to be sympathetic to his pleas of innocence. She was going to question him, put the pressure on, use what evidence she had, and take him to the point where he was willing to confess.

"I didn't do it," he said again. He was sobbing now, his shoulders heaving. "You don't believe me," he said, wiping at his face. "But I didn't do it."

This was a very different man from the one who had pointed the gun at himself, saying he wanted to escape his wretched guilt.

"Let's establish the facts for a start," she said. "Were you at the post-prom party, late on Saturday night?"

"Yes." He nodded, looking miserable. "I was there."

May's eyes widened. She hadn't known for sure that any of the school staff were there at all. This was a big surprise to her.

"Were you there in any official role? Were you there in your teacher's capacity?"

He shook his head again. "There were a few of us who just - who just came along after the prom. To hang out with the students, to have a drink. I mean, it was legitimate. We just wanted to join in the fun." He stared at her anxiously.

"Who else did you see?" May didn't trust his explanation at all.

"Uh, one or two others. I think Miss Jones was there. She teaches art. I noticed one or two others."

May concluded that very few teachers had been at the party, and that Coach Adamson, for some reason, had not been in a state to recognize or remember who else had shown up. Perhaps he'd been avoiding them. Or perhaps his focus had been elsewhere.

"So you were there, and you saw the girls, and you spoke to them?"

"Yes, that's all it was. Friendly. Caring."

"How did you get there?"

"I drove." That was all he said, and then looked away from her.

"Did you arrive before Sadie and Alyssa?"

"I – I don't know." He looked miserable, and wouldn't meet her eyes. "Maybe. I wasn't really paying attention. I just wanted to keep an eye on the kids. Make sure they were okay. Make sure no one got hurt or anything."

"So you were at the party just to socialize and look out for everyone?" That sure had gone wrong, May thought.

"Yeah. I was there." He made a vague gesture. "And I hung out with a few people, one on one. We talked about their careers, about life and stuff. That's it. Just friendly conversations."

"What time did you arrive?"

"The prom ended at about eleven. I think I probably got here about half past."

"What time did you leave?"

He paused, then said, "Sometime around three, maybe. I don't remember specifically."

"Did you see Sadie and Alyssa at any point during the evening?"

"Yeah. Sure, I think I even said hi. I mean, I honestly didn't see a problem. I can't understand how this happened. Everyone was getting along. People were dancing, socializing."

"Did anyone notice you speaking to Sadie or Alyssa?"

"I - I guess so. I don't remember."

"Did you tell anyone you were leaving?"

"I said goodbye to a couple of people. Everyone was pretty drunk by then."

"Did you drive straight home? Which route did you take?"

"I don't - I don't have a memory of that."

May's eyes widened. No memory of getting home? How drunk had he been? Or was he going to use this as an excuse, to say he'd had memory loss and couldn't take responsibility for the crimes?

"Oh?" She looked at him. "You don't remember anything about the drive home?"

"No. I'd had more alcohol than I meant to, and I was pretty tired. I remember thinking I should drive slowly, because I was feeling drunk, so as not to cause a crash. But that's about it."

"I see. So you're admitting to a DUI, for a start?" she challenged him.

"I don't recall exactly how much I'd had to drink," he said uneasily, flushing red.

"And there's a span of time here, from when you left the party to when you arrived home, that's missing from your memory?"

"Uh, yeah. That's correct."

"And you don't have a memory of what happened in that space of time?"

"No. I don't."

"Do you remember going into the woods before you left?"

"I don't remember. I don't think I did. I know at some stage, before I left, took a walk around the perimeter because I thought I'd lost my car keys, but then I found them in my inside pocket."

"Did you see Dylan, Alyssa's boyfriend, at all?"

"I definitely saw him but I can't recall when. Quite late, I think."

"Did you see him going into the woods?"

"That I don't recall."

"Did anyone see you arriving home?"

"No, I live alone. And like I said, I was driving slowly. I wouldn't have made a noise."

May shook her head. This was a very unreliable and piecemeal account. Coach Adamson could have strangled Alyssa during an alcohol-induced psychotic break. Or he could be giving deliberately vague and evasive answers. Either way, there was no clear alibi here and from that perspective, he was looking guilty.

Now it was time to find out what he'd done in the morning.

"What were your movements the next day? Early Sunday?" she asked.

"Early Sunday. I slept. I woke up feeling rough. I went for a run."

"You went for a run? Where?"

May recalled that, according to the map, Coach Adamson lived about five miles from the second murder site. A fit man, going for a run, could easily have gotten there on foot.

"I - I can show you the route, I think. I took a lot of the trails and they're quite complicated. I was feeling hungover."

"What time was that?"

"About - um - mid-morning, I think. We got a message, that's right. We got a message saying there had been an incident, and that all sporting events were canceled at school for Sunday afternoon and would be rescheduled for a later date. So after that message, I went for a run."

"And you can't trace the route on a map?"

"I would have difficulty doing that."

"Did you see anyone out running?"

"I don't know, I wasn't paying attention to anyone. I'm sure there were a few other people along the way. I think I saw a couple of walkers, and maybe one or two other runners."

May stared at him. "Could you recognize any of the other people? Did you see anyone you recognized? Did you greet anyone along the way?"

"No."

"Did you see Sadie Croft at any time during your run? Did you pass her house?"

"Her house?" He narrowed his eyes. "Yes, my running route goes past her house. She lives near one of the trail heads by the lake. But I didn't see her there. I mean, I didn't even think of that till now."

"Did you speak or communicate with anyone during the day?" May then asked.

"I messaged the football training group, making sure they knew about the change in the training time. And then in the late afternoon, I chatted with a few students online. I went to the grocery store, but that was later. At about six p.m. Picked up some food, had an early dinner, and turned in. Then much later in the evening, I got a message from the principal, saying that there had been a second student killed and that we were going to have a staff meeting at eight a.m. to discuss this serious issue. So I moved the morning training forward so it would be finished by then."

Again, the alibi was all but nonexistent. Clearly, not a single person could account for Coach Adamson's time that day.

May was satisfied he would have had the opportunity to murder both girls, and in fact had been in the local area when both had died.

So from that standpoint, their case was looking strong.

Now, she wanted to explore the reasons for his extreme reaction when he'd seen the officers come after him at training earlier.

"When we approached you at the training ground, you reacted violently. You attempted assault. You fled the scene. And you ended up in your office wielding a firearm. Why?"

Adamson hung his head.

"I - I thought you had probably found out about my past. You know, it occurred to me last night, that with these murders, they'd be looking into people's backgrounds and you might discover what I'd done. I never thought you would think I was the killer!" He stared at her, agonized and innocent-looking. "I thought you'd just come to arrest me for impersonating someone when I had a record."

"That was a very extreme reaction, given that we said we wanted to speak to you in connection with the murders."

"I was worried!"

"So you reacted by running away and ending up brandishing a firearm?"

"I panicked!" Adamson's voice was rising. "Where the hell else was I supposed to go?"

"You didn't think of just cooperating?"

"I know it was a stupid thing to do. I wanted to hide. I didn't know what to do. I'd done something terrible. I was ashamed."

He was practically crying again.

"And the firearm?"

"I - I'd gotten it a while ago, just for self-defense. I'm not violent. I do carry it with me to school. I keep it locked away in the locker, not on my person."

Now it was time for the most critical part of the questioning.

"Those photos of the girls in your car. When did you take them? Why did you print them out? Why those two girls?"

He stared at her.

"Photos? What are you talking about?"

"I am talking about this."

May showed him the shots she'd taken of the incriminating evidence. She hoped that this would crack right through his denial.

But instead, the coach turned pale.

"I didn't take those. I know nothing about them!" he said. "Did you plant those there? Are you trying to frame me for this?" He was breathing hard. "I refuse to answer any more questions. This is a setup. I want my lawyer. I need to call my lawyer. Now!"

May stood up.

This was a stumbling block, but it could hopefully be overcome. After all, Owen had just been going through the man's media, and she was sure that this would have included the image files. With any luck, they could get past this denial and then move forward with the questioning by showing him evidence to contradict what he was saying.

"I'm going to step outside for a few minutes. You need to calm down, Mr. Adamson. Calm down and think about your answers."

She'd come back with more concrete proof to break through this shield of denial. They really couldn't afford to mess this up.

May hurried outside to speak to Owen, hoping that his work would bring the final elements they needed to seal this case.

CHAPTER TWENTY SIX

When May rushed out of the interview room, she almost collided with Owen.

Hastily, she stepped back, feeling suddenly flustered, noticing he was doing the same.

"Sorry," he muttered.

"No problem," she said.

They stood for a moment, staring at each other. May mentally shook herself. She'd been strangely distracted there for a beat or two.

"He's denying any knowledge of the photos," she seethed to him.

"But they were in his car!" Owen said.

"He's saying the police planted them there."

Now, May saw Owen was looking worried, although she had no idea why.

"But why would we plant them there? How would we even have taken them? We weren't on the scene before the victims were killed," Owen protested.

"It's what he's saying. What he's claiming. But hopefully, it won't be an issue if there's enough evidence on his phone and hopefully, also in his messages."

Now, May's heart sank as she saw Owen was looking decidedly uneasy. He was looking down, shifting from foot to foot.

"You know, it's weird, but there were no images of the girls in his media," Owen confessed.

"What? How can that be?" May was horrified.

"I don't know. I checked all his media for evidence. Every single app I could access. And the laptop. There were no images of those girls anywhere. There were other photos, group shots, social pics, some training shots. Lots of photos. Just not those."

"But there have to be! Those shots were clearly recent. I mean, it was spring, and sunny, in them!"

"I'm telling you, there's nothing on here!" Owen said.

May stared at him. She felt boxed in. Walls were closing in on her.

"But what about his texts?" she said.

"There wasn't really anything incriminating on his phone. I mean, I didn't find anything." Owen looked up to meet her eyes. "There was hardly anything that I could show you at all. A few flirty messages. Definitely inappropriate, but not direct solicitation and not only to those two girls. That was it."

May stared at him.

"This can't be right!"

"I'm telling you, there's nothing."

May felt completely at a loss. "That's not possible. I know you've looked, but is there any way he could be hiding them? Maybe in an app that we don't have access to?"

"I guess so. Maybe a secret or hidden app. But in that case, we'd need to get the phone forensically analyzed."

May's heart sank. She knew what that meant.

Time.

Lots and lots of waiting time. The phone would need to be sent off to the specialists, and they always had a waitlist. Always. Usually a couple of weeks. Sometimes more.

Bitterly, she knew that the FBI could get this kind of thing done practically overnight. Kerry's cases had proved that to her time and again. But she was not in the same lucky situation here.

"I also thought he might have deleted them," Owen said.

"I guess he could have done that," May agreed. "Do you really think he would have, though? Knowing what they meant to him, deep inside?"

"Yes, I also have a problem with that. A guy like this, he would have wanted to save them somewhere. And he didn't email them anywhere or there would have been a record; I did check that carefully. We can search his house. Perhaps there's a storage device at his home where he keeps them. Or maybe he took them off a camera, or a second phone. Maybe he has a burner phone he uses just for that."

May nodded.

"I think we're going to need to do that search urgently, Owen. Can you go and organize it?"

"Yes, I'll take a couple of officers along with me. Are you going to go in for another round of questioning?"

May sighed. "Yes, I am. But I really don't know what direction to take now. I feel like we're stalled."

"We need to do something to get him to crack," Owen emphasized.

"Do you think we should inform him that we're going to search his house? I might be able to pick up something from his reaction."

Briefly, May felt comforted that in the pressure of this unexpected situation, she and Owen felt as close as ever. That awkwardness of earlier had gone away. Hopefully soon those scorching memories would also fade. She longed for things to be back the way they had been.

Then the side thought vanished, and the inexorable pressure of the case weighed down again.

Owen paused. Then he said, "I think so. I mean, if he's innocent, he'd want to be helpful, right? He wouldn't mind us searching. And if he's guilty he might give a sign. It might panic him."

May nodded. "Yeah, he'd want to be helpful if he was innocent. But I am finding his behavior so hard to read. He's so emotionally distraught. He teeters between appearing totally innocent, and being entirely guilty and with no hope of getting out of it. And just as I think - great, we're there, he goes the other way. This whole denying the photos and demanding his lawyer. Where did that even come from? Why?"

Could he have been telling the truth the whole way along?

May's mind grappled with that thought, but it was very far-fetched. For a start, it would have meant someone had planted that evidence in the car. Who would have done that? It was simply impossible. Every time she considered that theory, stumbling blocks seemed to spike out of the ground every way she looked.

The car had been unlocked, though. There was that. But May guessed that in a secure parking lot, in this small school, it was likely that teachers would be careless with the actual locking of their cars.

"Well, we'll just have to see what happens when he finds out that we're doing a search."

"Right," May said. "Right. I'll head back in there and do another round of questioning."

"I hope we get some results," Owen said. "I'll let you know as soon as possible. I'll call you the minute we find anything."

He rushed off.

May drew a deep breath, trying to get the emotional strength she needed to go back in that room to verbally fence with this anguished, guilty man again.

As she got up from the desk, Sheriff Jack walked in.

"May. There you are. I'm glad I caught you before you went back into the interview room. I guess we have not yet had a full confession from the suspect?"

May looked up, feeling hopeful. Sheriff Jack had been keeping things together, running everything in the county while they'd been chasing the killer. Perhaps he, too, had come across something that could be helpful.

"Not yet. He's close, but he's denying very important points. Owen just left to search his house. Is there anything you have discovered that we can use?"

Although, looking at him closely, he didn't look exactly thrilled by what he was about to tell her.

"I have some unexpected news," Jack said. "A few of the teachers at the school are waiting here in the police department's lobby. I think three have come along."

May's eyes widened. "Why's that?"

"They said they would like to give their input and answer questions. They just want to try to do the right thing for the students. But it might be that one of them has come across incriminating evidence, or a student has told them something in confidence. No students have come forward. The school called me and told me. So it's possible one of the teachers is here to act as a proxy."

"That's definitely possible," May said.

"I think you should talk to them immediately. Maybe that's our next step. It's going to be important to get their testimony before you interview Adamson again."

"That could get us further," May agreed. She was feeling distinctly flat about the case. Interviewing the teachers might take a lot of time, but if it gave her the fragment of a lead, it could be helpful in her next showdown with Coach Adamson.

"I'll take Adamson down to the holding cells. You can use the interview room. Make sure to ask the teachers about the interactions with the students, and if they noticed any untoward engagement between them and the suspect."

May felt as if there was now a ray of hope in the case. She was sure that one of the students had shared something in confidence with a teacher. And, with these kind people having come forward to volunteer, they might just learn a shocking truth.

CHAPTER TWENTY SEVEN

May watched at the police department's side entrance as Sheriff Jack, together with one of the other police, escorted Coach Adamson down to the cells. She hoped that some time down there would allow him to rethink and decide that it was better to give up on his denial.

But she was more hopeful about the different strategies they now had, that might prove his guilt circumstantially.

Owen was already on the way to his house, to do a search for any hidden storage devices or other concealed evidence.

And three teachers were lined up, having voluntarily come forward to offer their testament in this tragic case. May felt incredibly thankful that they had taken the time to do this. These teachers must have information they thought would be important.

Hopefully it would be enough to plug the holes in this case that seemed to be causing it to leak again and again.

The sergeant at the desk was busy processing these witnesses, taking their names and details, before escorting them to the interview room.

Hearing footsteps approach the interview room, May turned and hurried back inside. She needed to get these interviews concluded as soon as possible. The community was restless, angry, and seeking answers. They had to press the charges as soon as possible, but May deeply feared that a flawed case might sink them.

As the new deputy for Tamarack County, she did not want that on her record. It would be disastrous.

The responsibility was a lead weight on her shoulders as she stepped into the room, sure that Sheriff Jack would be feeling exactly the same. May realized she'd learned a lot of her work ethics and values from her boss, who embodied integrity.

If only everyone was like him! But instead, they were dealing on a constant basis with people who lied, people who made up stories and concealed facts and created false scenarios either for their own benefit, or to take someone else down.

Sometimes, May despaired about humanity, although she had to admit that in her community, more of what happened did end up restoring her faith in it.

However, she knew that even though she suspected Coach Adamson might be lying and was concealing very pertinent information on this case, it could also be that others would do the same. Some people might have a motive for wanting to take the coach down.

She would have to carefully analyze each of these testimonies, and ensure that she tested their versions just as thoroughly as she'd tested the suspect's.

Having given herself this short but important pep talk, May stepped into the room, coming face to face with a young, dark haired, wide-eyed woman with an earnest expression.

"Good morning," she greeted her with a warm nod. "I'm Deputy Moore."

"Yes, I know," the teacher said. "I'm Gwendoline Evans and I used to be taught by your mom. Mrs. Moore! She was so awesome. She taught me math, science, and history. She brought the past world alive for me. In fact, she's one of the reasons I was inspired to become a teacher."

"That's wonderful," May said. She'd heard lots of tributes like that about her mom. It always made her feel proud, but at the same time, as if she could never fill her shoes adequately.

"So I thought it was my duty to give testimony," Gwendoline said. "I don't know if my story will be helpful, but if it helps solve this crime, I'll be very happy."

"We're investigating every possibility," May told her. "Any details will be helpful to us."

"I was at the school on Friday, the day before the prom, and I saw something that might be important. I'd like to share it with you."

"Please go on," May said.

"It was toward the end of the day, and students were rushing out. I was in my office, just wrapping up some things, and I heard a commotion from the hallway. It took me a moment to realize it was the suspect who I now know to be Coach Adamson. He was arguing with two other teachers, and taking them to task for something."

"I see," said May. "And what was it about?"

"That's the thing," Gwendoline said. "It was a bit hard to hear, but it was definitely something. I heard the word 'discipline', and 'unprofessional.' There was definitely something going on."

"You didn't hear more?"

"I couldn't tell exactly," Gwendoline said. "But he was berating them, and calling them some pretty bad names. The two teachers were trying to placate him, but it was clear that he was really angry about something. Then, he turned on his heel and stormed out of the building."

"Who were the teachers?"

"They were the two assistants who had been handling the sports classes on some weekends."

"So would you say that Coach Adamson had been angry with them for a lack of discipline?"

"Perhaps, yes," Gwendoline said, now looking confused. "I'm not sure exactly what that whole confrontation meant. But it definitely meant he could lose his temper."

May nodded, careful to make sure she looked appreciative.

"Thank you. And was there anything else? Any students that shared anything with you?"

"No, no. My students all seem to be happy with their P.E. classes. But that one incident was bothering me."

"What was your personal opinion of Coach Adamson?" she asked.

"I never liked him. I always felt that something about him was off. I don't know why. Maybe it was that he always tried to be too friendly, in a creepy way."

"Anything you noticed him say or do that would confirm that?"

"I'm sure there were lots of small things. Ultimately, it was the way he made me feel, though. My instincts, I guess." She shrugged.

"I really appreciate this information," May said again.

As Gwendoline got up and left, she fervently hoped that the next witnesses had more concrete facts. When it came to people, anything was possible.

The next teacher into the room was an older, gray-haired man.

"Good morning, deputy," he said as soon as he walked into the room. He took a seat and stared at her gravely.

"Good morning," May said.

"I am Sam Hampshire, the deputy head of English and arts, and I am extremely concerned by what has been happening in this school."

"Please explain more," May said, wondering if this would go somewhere, or end up being as inconclusive as Gwendoline's information had been.

"For the last six months or so, I have felt something is wrong. I haven't been able to pinpoint why. But as a teacher with a career spanning thirty-five years, twenty at this school, I think I know it well enough to feel when something is amiss. There was something off-kilter in our staff relationships."

May hoped he would be able to voice his feelings more clearly. Why six months, she wondered. What had happened in that timeframe?

"Did you suspect Coach Adamson in particular?" she asked. "Was there any incident, either now or else six months ago, that made you feel differently about him?"

Sam thought carefully, resting his chin on his hands.

"There seemed to be a lot of unpleasantness going around in the past few months. I felt the atmosphere at the school had changed, but I couldn't put my finger on it. There were strange facts coming out about people. Rumors circulating, some of which proved to be true. We even had one staff member resign a few weeks ago. He was a very well liked teacher. Mr. Hartley, who taught science. Something came to light about exam papers with a failing grade that he'd overlooked last term. I'm not sure if it was a genuine mistake or not, but he left all the same."

May nodded. This was interesting information. Had this teacher come back to commit the crimes? It was a long shot but she needed to check.

"Do you know where Mr. Hartley went?" she asked.

"He quit teaching completely, I believe. He has family in Washington, and he moved there to work in their business."

That ruled him out as a suspect, May knew.

"Did you receive any complaints from students? Any feedback from them at all, regarding Coach Adamson, or anything else of concern?" she then checked.

"No, not from students. I personally thought everyone did their best to keep the toxic dynamic from the students, even though some of them probably picked up on it."

"Thank you so much for this," May said gratefully, as Sam nodded before standing up and walking out.

This gave her a lot of food for thought.

Something had happened in the last six months that she guessed might have triggered Coach Adamson to change into what he had become - a brutal killer.

This gave them an additional reason to relook at his life. May knew that sometimes even small things could precipitate a psychopath to start killing.

A minor incident, a fight, another crime. Perhaps a relationship had broken up, or someone that had been close to him or a stabilizing influence had died, or parted ways with him. There were a myriad of factors that could precipitate a serial killing spree in somebody who had always had the potential to become a killer.

But the six-month mark was interesting. With one more interview to conduct, May wondered if other testimonies would add to this compelling weight of evidence.

Perhaps this next teacher would be able to offer more facts, May wondered, as her final interviewee stepped inside the room.

CHAPTER TWENTY EIGHT

The final teacher to walk into May's interview room was a shy-looking man, with short, brown hair and an anxious expression. He looked to be in his mid-thirties, May thought.

"Good morning. I'm Deputy Moore. Thank you for coming forward," she said.

"Good morning. I'm Mr. York, and I'm a math and science teacher. I teach students from sixth to twelfth grade."

"Please, sit," May said. "What information would you like to share?"

York sat. He looked uncomfortable and worried.

"Please understand that I am not a very brave man," York said with a rueful smile. He was clearly uncomfortable speaking in front of a police officer. "I apologize for being nervous. But this is a very big deal for the school. And it's a very big deal for me. I don't really like coming forward this way, but I felt I needed to, to support the school and the students."

"I appreciate that," May said.

"I personally noticed Coach Adamson on a few occasions, displaying what I thought was inappropriate behavior toward students. Taking photos of them. Speaking in a flirtatious manner."

"Any particular students?"

"I noticed him - well, I can only describe it as stalking - Alyssa. I didn't notice him stalking Sadie, but she was less involved in school activities and more of a loner, I think."

"When was this?" May asked.

"I've been noticing it for a couple of weeks now. I think what intrigued me was that he seemed to be using a different phone to take the photos."

"Is that so?" May asked, her adrenaline spiking. This would explain the absence of them on the camera gallery.

"Yes. I watched him one day, taking a different phone out of his pocket, and I thought how strange that was. But then, you know, I sadly thought no more of it. How I wish now that I'd spoken up and said something at the time."

"I'm glad we have this information now," May said. She felt a huge relief. A piece of the puzzle - an important piece - had been filled in.

"Did you have any testimonies from any students?" May asked. "Did anyone reach out to you and say they felt uneasy?"

"No, nobody did. I think the way he did things was too discreet. But there is one thing troubling me," York said.

"What is that?" May asked, now feeling concerned.

"I'm sure I saw him taking photos of one of the other girls."

"Which girl was that?"

York shook his head. "I've been trying my hardest to remember who it was. It was such a fleeting glimpse and I was distracted at the time. But I think it's important. What if - I have had nightmares about this ever since you picked him up this morning - what if he already took a third victim, and you haven't discovered it yet? I mean, it was sheer chance that the second victim was discovered, in such an out of the way place. Those trails are very remote."

That awful reality thudded down on May like a lead weight. This was a terrible thought, and she had to admit, it was a possibility. Not everyone at the school was accounted for. A lot of people had stayed home after the murders. As yet, if one person had gone missing early this morning, that person might not yet have been picked up on.

"We'll be sure to ask about that," she said, now unable to shake the cold feeling in her stomach. "I will do my best to make sure everyone is accounted for. And this has been a very helpful interview. I will probably need to contact you again."

"That's no problem," he said.

"And I will ask again, did anybody else reach out to you or other teachers, who might have been feeling uneasy about Coach Adamson's behavior?"

York thought for a moment.

"No. I'm sure I would have remembered."

May was thinking hard about all the possible identities of a potential third victim. She felt a queasy, sick feeling in her stomach.

"The police will do everything they can to make sure everyone is accounted for," May said with more confidence than she actually felt, as her mind swirled with possibilities.

If Adamson had been stealthy enough to take a victim without anyone noticing, they might not have realized they'd gone missing yet.

Another murder. It was a possibility. She hated to admit it, but it was possible. It might be a long shot, but there was nobody else to check. The serial killer might have already struck again.

That might also have accounted for his extreme guilty reaction when the police had arrived, she thought, icy fingers running down her spine.

"Thank you. And thank you for taking the time to speak with me." She tried to keep her voice brisk and professional even though she felt sick inside.

"Thank you," York said. "I meant what I said. I'm not a brave man. I can't tell you how hard it was to even come here and say these things, but I felt I had to do my part to make the students safe."

But, as York got up, May remembered there was one more piece of information she needed. She'd been so shaken by what he'd told her that it had flown out of her head for a moment.

"Oh, another question," she said. "In the last six months, did you notice any change in the dynamic among the staff? Anything untoward, any individual causing trouble?"

He shook his head.

"I only joined the team at the start of this year, so I wouldn't have had any knowledge of what it was like here previously," he said.

"Okay. No problem. Thank you for the information. Please will you sign a statement at the front desk before you leave?"

"I will do that."

He got up from the desk.

May watched the teacher walk to the door. She felt sick with apprehension. Her mind was racing. She'd never had to deal with a case like this before.

What if there was a third victim? What if he'd already killed? That would mean that there was nothing she could do. It would be too late.

How could they find out who else he had been following and photographing?

She felt a deep fear. She felt an overwhelming sense of dread.

She had no idea where to start.

And she was certain that, if Adamson had indeed struck again, the police were already too late to save another victim.

Breathing deeply, May knew panicking wouldn't help her now. In fact, it would count against her. All she could do was follow the evidence, the facts, and hope that no matter whether Adamson had already killed again or not, they had what they needed to put him away for life.

And, at that moment, as he reached the door, York turned around.

His face was alight.

"I've remembered who it was," he said. "It was a student called Berenice Thom. She lives on the other side of Sleepy Hollow. I didn't see her at school today so I guess her parents must have kept her home. I hope so, anyway."

"Thank you," May said, rushing for the phone.

CHAPTER TWENTY NINE

May dialed the Thoms' home number, feeling sick with tension. Let the victim be home and safe, she prayed. Let her be alright.

It felt like eons before the call was picked up.

"Mrs. Thom speaking?" a woman's voice said.

"Mrs. Thom, it's Deputy Moore here," May said, doing her best to keep her voice calm. "We're calling about your daughter, Berenice."

"What about her? Is she alright?" the mother asked anxiously.

May felt her stomach churn.

"Is she not at home?"

"No. She walked to school early. On Mondays, she usually trains at the school gym before class. Why? What's gone wrong?"

"Your daughter is not at school," May told her with a sense of terrible finality. "We've just checked with the principal's office, and she never arrived this morning. They took a detailed roll call, as a result of what's been going on. Please, can you give us her cellphone number? We need to see if we can locate her urgently."

Mrs. Thom sounded panicked. "Her phone won't help you. She leaves it at home. I don't allow her to take it to school, as it disrupts her focus, and the school is only a couple of miles away. Where's my daughter?" Her voice was frantic now. "How can we find her? How can we find my daughter?"

May rushed to the door of the interview room. This was the most terrible scenario she could have imagined. A life was at stake. A girl was missing.

And the monster who had taken her, who had most likely killed her, had said nothing about this.

Nothing at all.

May felt appalled. How were they going to get the truth out of him? This could turn into the most protracted, drawn out case. It might never end in closure for the Thoms. Imagine if this woman was only ever listed as 'missing,' just like Lauren had been? There were plenty of places in the more rural areas where a body could be dumped and not found for decades, if at all.

If only she could figure out a way to make Coach Adamson tell the truth. But admitting he'd killed a third woman would only add to his guilt.

Could Owen find any evidence in the coach's house? That was a possibility.

If Owen had found anything at all, she knew he would call instantly. That was what had been arranged. He was already on the lookout for anything suspicious, any other phone, any signs. But she could remind him.

She dialed his number, feeling breathless with tension and fear.

"May," he said almost immediately. "Do you have a confession yet?"

Her heart sank.

"No. And we need evidence, more than ever. It's likely he may have taken and killed a third victim."

"Who's that?" Owen asked, anxiety now radiating from his voice.

"A student called Berenice Thom. Please, look out for any communication from her. Any hints as to where he might have taken her. For the time being, I'm going to meet with Sheriff Jack, and see what we can come up with in terms of a strategy that might get Coach Adamson to tell the truth."

Feeling on the point of tears, May cut the call. She paused and leaned against the wall of the police station.

She forced herself to breathe deeply. Being upset and anxious would not help her now. She needed to carefully and calmly review the evidence, thinking clearly about what she had been told. That was always what Sheriff Jack told her. No matter how tense the situation, clear thought would always show the way forward.

But this woman could be anywhere. Dumped on one of the many isolated trails. She remembered York's words during the interview.

Then, with a cold shock, May realized what had been wrong with those words. She actually gasped aloud as the conclusion came to her.

"Seriously?" she whispered. "Seriously?"

Reviewing the facts, her mind spinning, she now found herself coming up with an odd alternative scenario. What if she'd been looking at everything totally the wrong way?

It was weird, she thought. Once she'd seen the possibility, she couldn't unsee it. Once she'd looked at how the facts fitted together, she saw that they could also fit in another way. A completely different way.

Now, she felt totally torn.

She couldn't shake off the horrible feeling that she'd been led astray in this case.

And if that was the case, if the ultimate conclusion led where she feared, then what she dreaded the most might not have happened yet.

Now, May turned and marched to the police department's exit door. She didn't want to go back into the interview room yet.

Not until she'd properly thought through the alternative scenario that had just occurred to her.

She might be wrong. She might be misinterpreting something. But if she was right, there was no time to lose. Not when the nondescript gray Chevy, at this very moment, was already driving carefully out of the parking lot after York had finalized and signed his statement at the front desk.

What to do?

Giving in to her policewoman's instincts, May grabbed her car keys and rushed out of the police department, jumping into her own car which was not a police cruiser and could drive the roads unnoticed, like a normal citizen's.

As she jumped into the car, she tried to make coherent sense of her instinctive reaction. She ran the facts through her mind, acknowledging the inconsistencies.

Firstly, it was in what York had noticed, and what he hadn't.

He'd noticed a second phone! May had been stunned when she'd heard that. Those were some serious observation skills, right there. She'd been impressed. Not many people could pick up that kind of thing when observing a random colleague.

But this same observant person had not been able to name the third student he'd said that Coach Adamson had been photographing.

Not until right at the end of the interview when he was about to leave.

And then, May thought about the photos which had so conveniently turned up in Adamson's car, just after the police had arrived to take him in for questioning. Would he really have left them there, in full view on the passenger seat? After concealing all other evidence, including the burner phone?

As May drove down the road, those were the first issues that seethed in her mind. But there were others. There was more.

There was the question of timing.

More than one of the teachers had talked about the change in dynamic that had occurred about six months ago. They hadn't really been able to explain it. Things had soured and gone bad. Information had been circulating that placed some people in a negative light.

A popular teacher had resigned after evidence had come to light against him.

This indicated that something had changed in that timeframe. Something, or someone, had started to influence the environment and it had become toxic.

She'd asked York about it and he'd said he'd only joined at the start of the year and hadn't known what things were like.

But the start of the year was just over six months ago. What if he'd been the one to change things?

What if his arrival had made everything different?

Now, May knew that all of this was mere supposition. And in fact, she would have brushed it aside, if it were not for the final and most troubling inconsistency in the story, the one that had only leaped into her mind as she reviewed the evidence, and which she most definitely could not explain.

Keeping a few cars behind the Chevy, May watched intently as he turned a corner. Where was he going?

Discreetly, she eased around the bend, following. She really didn't want him to see her. Not when a life might depend on it.

The final issue was that he'd talked about the second victim being discovered in such an out of the way place. "Those trails are very remote," he'd said.

But to May's knowledge, as yet, the whereabouts of Sadie Croft had not been made public. The crime scene had not been disclosed and in fact, because it was such a remote location, they deliberately had not made this common knowledge.

And yet, York had spoken about it with familiarity. As if he knew exactly where the place was. Of course, there was a chance he'd managed to hear through the grapevine, small towns being what they were. But maybe, too, there was another, more obvious reason why he knew where it was. And that reason was that he himself had followed Sadie there, and killed her.

All of that had a very important bearing on the other thing he'd said, and May gripped the wheel as she remembered that bombshell.

He'd said that he thought the coach might have had time to take another victim.

But thinking ahead, May wondered if this was maybe just laying the groundwork for what he had planned, except the police arrived too soon.

So maybe, by saying this, he was setting the scene for another body to be discovered, supposedly killed by Coach Adamson, in a remote place, a few days from now, when the exact time of death might be difficult to establish.

Only, the final victim hadn't been killed yet, because he hadn't had time. Instead, he was on his way to commit the murder now. And by dropping that bombshell, he'd made very sure that the police would all be swarming around Adamson, trying to get the truth from him, leaving him free and clear to go and find Berenice himself. They wouldn't expect him back at school for a while, since he was the last to be interviewed.

May let out a traumatized sigh.

It was as if she was looking at things from two totally different angles. Was she completely right or was she embarrassingly wrong?

She shook her head. This was all conjecture. She had no actual proof.

But if she was right, then she was doing what she needed to do. Of course, if she was right, then she might also be putting herself in danger. But she had to find out more.

What did she really know about York?

She'd been so impressed by his story. Until those little details starting nagging at her cop's mind. But beyond that, he'd shown an alarming talent for being convincing. He'd come across as sincere. A humble, everyday man stepping up to the plate when it mattered. And the awful thing is, that could be who he really was.

As she watched, York made another turn.

He might be heading back to the school. If he was heading back to the school, then he was surely innocent.

The next minute would be the deciding factor.

May turned along with him, keeping a couple of hundred yards behind, counting down the moments that would help to prove York's innocence, or his guilt.

CHAPTER THIRTY

May felt as if her hands were welded to the wheel as she waited to see which way York would turn. Thoughts were racing through her mind. She veered again and again between thinking she was right, and being sure that she was following a mad theory that was just wasting time.

And then York turned onto the secondary road that wound its way down to Sleepy Hollow School, and May felt her tension ebb away. It was okay. She'd been wrong, but it had still been a very important lead to check out.

Now she could turn back, rush to the police department, and plunge straight into her interrogation of Coach Adamson, so that they could find out where the third victim had been dumped, and bring the family closure.

But, at that moment, as May was slowing down for her turn, the Chevy sped up and darted down a side road that led in the opposite direction of the school grounds.

"It is him! It is!" May yelled.

Correcting her course, she flattened her foot, desperate now to catch up with him because he was suddenly driving faster.

He was off on a mission, that was clear. He'd totally changed his driving style. Now he was accelerating along, swerving around the bends of the narrow, winding road that led out of town, skirting the woods and the lake. Perhaps he was doing that because he thought he was alone and unobserved, and he was in a hurry to get where he was going.

May got on the phone to Owen. She had to tell him what was happening, and at the same time she had to keep the car in sight.

He picked up immediately, to her relief.

"News?" he said.

"Yes," May replied breathlessly. "I'm following a suspect."

"What?" Owen asked, astonished. "Another suspect?"

"The math teacher," May said. "Mr. York. It was him all along. I think he's taken the third victim somewhere already. And he's going to find her now and kill her."

"May! Where are you headed?"

"I don't know where he's going. He's taking a back road going north out of Sleepy Hollow. I might lose him," she said. This was turning into such a disaster. What if she didn't catch him at all? He was driving like a demon now.

"You won't lose him. You're a brilliant driver. Send me the location as soon as you can. As soon as he stops. In the meantime, I'll get on the road to Sleepy Hollow so that I'm in the area."

She cut the call, feeling grateful for Owen's reassurance, which had bolstered her confidence and given her the will to speed around these hairpin bends as York headed into the hills.

It was a balancing act that required hanging back enough to avoid being seen, but staying close enough to be able to follow him, as he weaved in and out of the forest, and then out along a dirt track, where it was clear he had driven before, for his driving seemed very confident and sure.

May was starting to sweat with the effort of keeping up, as she rounded yet another bend. If she lost him, she had no doubt at all that his victim would lose her life. This was the only chance she had to save the girl. This pressure was leaving her on the edge of her nerves. But she dug deep inside herself, and was surprised by the resilience and strength of will she discovered there.

She was going to catch this killer and bring an end to this terrifying string of murders. And she was determined to save Berenice, if she possibly could.

How she wished she'd been able to pick up at the police station what he was planning. But then again, he would just have denied it, and in any case, they had no proof at all, other than the connections May had made in her own mind. So this was the only way, dangerous and risky as it was. At least, with every turn they took, she felt surer that he had hidden the girl out here and was coming back.

She clung to the possibility that Berenice might still be alive, though she was certain he intended to kill her.

She just had to pray that she caught him.

Before it was too late.

There! He was stopping! May caught her breath.

With a squeal of tires, York swerved into a clearing. In a cloud of dust, he stopped the car. It was almost invisible from the road. If May hadn't seen the turn and the dust, she would never even have noticed the gray car, parked almost behind a clump of trees.

By the time she'd reached it, he had gone.

Quickly, May took a moment to send Owen the coordinates before jumping out of her car.

And then, she sped down the trail that led deep into the woods. He had to have gone this way. There was only one path he could take, though it was clearly seldom used, a route known only to him.

He must have come here earlier and brought her, dumped her.

Trying to be as quiet as she could, May headed deeper into the woods, dreading what she would find, knowing that backup would never get here in time for this confrontation, and it was only going to be her against him.

And then, ahead of her, she heard his voice.

It sent shivers down May's spine. He was speaking in a wheedling way, with an evil laugh in his words.

"Oh, my baby. You're my queen. I've saved you for last. Last and longest. You're the one I wanted the most. The one who's the most special to me. Show me your face, your beautiful face."

May heard sobbing and screaming, but the cries were muted. She thought the girl was simply too terrified to make a noise.

With her heart hammering violently, she crept forward along the stony, uneven trail, knowing that at any moment she would be in his sight. Then, she would have to take him down, on her own, not knowing what to expect.

May drew her gun. Her hand was trembling.

She stepped forward again. She couldn't delay. Those girls had been killed quickly, and with significant strength. If she was too slow, he might already have done the deed and caused fatal damage in just a few moments.

Taking a deep breath, May rushed forward.

There he was. On the other side of a large clearing, kneeling over the girl, who lay with her back against a tree, her hands and ankles tied. She was desperately struggling, her eyes wide.

"Step away from her! Hands in the air!" May yelled.

But he was too quick for her.

As May rushed toward him, York's face changed. It hardened into a snarl. With lightning speed, he grabbed the girl and pulled her in front of him.

Now she couldn't shoot. There was no clear shot. He was using Berenice, effectively, as a shield.

In a moment, the look on the teacher's face changed to one of pure rage. His mouth curled into a snarl, and his eyes narrowed.

"You," he hissed. "How did you find me?"

"Never mind that now," May insisted.

"Get back," he threatened her, hooking his hands around the girl's neck as she screamed in terror.

"You need to let her go. This is over now," May insisted. She was fighting for calmness, doing her best to think through the situation and figure out how she could get across the clearing to either free the girl, or get a clear shot at her captor.

"It is not over. I've only just started with her. But if you take one more step, I'll finish her!" he said.

May stopped. Her heart was pounding.

They were in a standoff which, at any moment, could turn deadly.

CHAPTER THIRTY ONE

May couldn't shoot. It was too risky. There wasn't enough of York's body visible behind the terrified girl. She simply couldn't aim at the narrow margin of head, the sliver of arm, that was all she had to go by.

Plus, if she missed, things would get extremely bad, very fast. It took only seconds to lose consciousness in this situation, and if there was enough damage done, the girl might not live. Her windpipe could easily be crushed. He might even break her neck. He was stronger than he looked. That average seeming, pinstripe shirt concealed bulky muscles and powerful arms, May now realized.

She had to talk him down. It had worked with Coach Adamson. It was a scary, precarious thing to do but it was her only option.

"Mr. York, this has gone way too far. You don't have to do this. Just let her go," May said.

"I can't," he argued back. "She's the one I need to kill the most."

At least she had him talking. But she didn't like what he was saying. Not at all.

"You can't kill her. She's a person. She has her whole life ahead of her. You can't do this," May insisted.

"You just don't get it," he said. With horror, May realized the evil man was smiling.

He gave a little shake of his head, but his hands didn't relax their grip on her. Not for one moment.

He was alert and aware. He was ready for her.

May had to get closer, somehow. Her time was limited. At any moment, he could tighten his grip and kill Berenice.

"Let her go, and I'll go with you. She's just a girl. There are others. There's no need to kill her," May offered.

"I want her. I want her more than any of the others. She's mine. She's been mine from the start."

Now May could see the madness in his eyes.

She had to try. She had to get him down. She had to have a clear shot. At any moment, he could crush the girl's throat. This was the only chance she had.

She edged forward, speaking again as she stepped to try and distract him from the fact.

"How did you do it? How did you get them to trust you?" May asked him, making sure to sound curious.

"Oh, I didn't have the same charisma as that coach." His voice was filled with disgust. "Or that other teacher. I got rid of him. I could see he was like flypaper to the girls."

May had wondered about the other teacher's sudden resignation and that odd scandal. So this had, in fact, been caused by York. He'd clearly applied his evil intelligence to obliterating what he considered as his 'competition.' She guessed that was why the coach had been framed. Maybe York had somehow learned, or just sensed, what his background was.

"I didn't have any of those qualities. All I had was knowledge. They trusted me because I knew things they didn't. But at the same time they scorned me because math is not exciting. All I had was specific information they needed, but didn't admire."

He sounded angry now.

"They thought I was a bore. A pedant. I was a geek, the guy they teased in high school. I knew how to do my job, but I had no charisma or charm. I didn't have any good stories."

May took another step toward him.

"That must have been difficult for you," she said.

"Still, I knew the right things to say to them. 'You have a future ahead of you,' I told them. 'Here are the opportunities I see for you,' I said."

"I see," May agreed.

"I'm smart! I'm smarter than any of the other teachers. But I couldn't bear the thought that these young women didn't see me for who I was. They just didn't see me! And so, they needed to die. Just as you will die, my sweetest queen."

He removed a hand, and stroked Berenice's hair.

It was the most vile act May had ever seen, as he caressed the woman's hair while she sobbed, her face a rictus of fear.

But it gave May the chance she needed.

He'd been distracted from his brutal hold on her and she'd gotten a little closer. This was her chance.

She leaped forward, sprinting across the remaining distance, and made a grab for his arm.

But he was fast. Terrifyingly fast. This monster had reactions far speedier than he should have possessed. Within a moment, he'd shoved the girl aside and grabbed May's gun hand.

She yelled aloud as he wrenched her gun viciously away. He tossed it into the undergrowth, invisible and hidden.

And then, in a moment, May was fighting for her life.

He had her by the wrist, trying to bend it back. She fought him with all her strength, but she was no match for him. His fingers were like steel, and they were digging into her flesh.

She gasped and tried to fight him off.

But he was too strong. He tightened his grip and forced her to the ground.

"This is your fault. You shouldn't have come here. You should have let me be," he accused, as he put all his weight onto her arm while he held her down, twigs digging into her skin. She felt a surge of terror as she imagined what the victims must have felt.

She tried to twist away, but he yanked her back. Desperately, May kicked out at him, hoping to make contact, to hurt him.

She heard him hiss as her foot connected with his leg, but there was no pause in his attack on her.

"You're strong. I'll give you that much. But you'll have to try harder than that," he taunted callously, as if he were talking about a math problem.

His hands were finding her neck now. Wrapping around her throat. She clawed at his fingers but it was as if he didn't even feel her.

"This won't take long. And then, I'll have my prom queen all to myself," he muttered. She could feel his breath on her cheek, his mouth inches from her face.

She felt incredibly frustrated, and filled with fear, that she was lighter, and less strong, than this thickset, brutal man. Berenice had not managed to go far. She'd writhed a yard or so away, but she was clearly paralyzed by shock and fear. She couldn't escape, not when she was tied so tight.

She wasn't going to be able to get away and was still at risk. If this man killed May, he would then murder Berenice. And he wanted to kill her. She could see the expectation in his face, the eagerness in his eyes.

But she had other skills, May reminded herself, refusing to give in to panic. With only a moment to go before he finished her, at the last possible second, she could only try trickery.

She looked up at him, her eyes wide.

"I'm sorry, I'm sorry, I'm sorry," she said, in a sobbing tone.

"You're sorry? You're sorry for what?" he demanded, sounding surprised.

She stayed silent, pretending she couldn't answer the question.

"Don't you know?" she whispered. "Can't you tell?"

"You're sorry for what?" he said, louder. But his grip on her throat had relaxed. She'd led his mind away from the focus of killing and bought herself the precious time she needed.

She opened her mouth to speak and then, as she did, she used every ounce of strength she had and head butted him.

Her forehead slammed into his nose and he cried out in pain.

In the same moment, she kicked out, trying to get distance between them. She was rewarded with his grip slipping and a moment of freedom. May gave a yell and kicked out with all her might, connecting with his ribs.

The blow was enough to make him stagger back.

May scrambled to her feet and kicked him again, aiming for the solar plexus, and she got lucky.

The breath choked out of him, and he doubled over, coughing.

This was it. Her only chance to make sure he stayed down. May didn't hesitate.

She kicked out at his head, her boot slamming into his skull.

He cried out and his body went limp. She thought the fight was ebbing from him. She leaped forward, only to find that his grabbing hand was ready to trap her again.

His fingers clawed at her wrist. He was still fighting. Still conscious, and she felt a sense of doom.

She bashed her fist into his neck, and then did it again, needing to choke him, giving it all the power that she had, doing it for Lauren. Fighting in a way she wished her sister had done. Battling for her life. She had him! Now she was grasping his wrist and he was the one coughing for breath.

And then, footsteps crashed into the clearing. May spun around as Owen burst through the trees, holding his gun.

"May! Are you alright?"

Panting, holding York down with all her strength, May nodded.

"I think I've gotten the better of him. But I could - I could use some help handcuffing him!" she gasped.

As Owen rushed forward to help, May felt dizzy and weak with utter relief.

This had been the closest margin of survival. She couldn't believe that, against all odds, she'd managed to capture the right criminal, and also save his final victim.

It had been touch and go. It could so easily have ended differently. She'd had to put herself at serious risk against a very skilled and extremely dangerous adversary.

But he would not terrorize the community any longer. Wiping mud from her hands, May scrambled up.

She had saved a life, and even though she was exhausted to the bone, that knowledge warmed her as she helped Berenice to her feet and began struggling with her ropes.

EPILOGUE

It was eight p.m. before May had finished all the paperwork that needed to be done, and the final interviews on the case were concluded. The evidence against York was overwhelming and May was satisfied that the case was iron hard. He would be in prison for life, a flawed yet highly intelligent psychopath who had chosen his move to the new school as the time to begin planning his murderous urges.

She put down her pen after signing the final document, feeling bone weary.

"Congratulations, May." Sheriff Jack hurried through from the lobby. "I've already had a number of the teachers coming back again here to say thanks, as well as the school principal. They all say that putting two and two together, the troubles at the school started when York arrived at the start of this year."

"I guess that's the kind of person he was. Manipulative and evil."

"Thankfully, now behind bars. As Coach Adamson will remain too, with lesser charges. For sure, our town's a safer place tonight. Well done to the both of you," he praised her. "You'd better knock off now. This has been a brutal case. You deserve some rest. If you're done here, go."

He turned to walk out and then turned back. "There are flowers for you in the lobby. Berenice's parents brought them. It's a lovely arrangement. Don't forget to take them with you when you leave."

"Thank you. I will," May said, feeling pleased and gratified.

And then she glanced across the desk at Owen, sitting opposite. He looked as if he wanted to say something, but had decided against it.

So May decided to take the initiative herself.

"I'm sorry for what happened earlier," she said, blushing crimson, knowing he knew exactly which 'earlier' she meant.

"That's no problem," he muttered.

"I misunderstood you. I – I'm sorry. So I'd like to make a suggestion."

"What's that?" Now Owen sounded surprised.

"Why don't we take a walk down to Dan's Bar before we head home?" she asked. "We could have a drink and a bite to eat. Maybe a burger."

Suddenly, May was craving a burger. And she didn't even care that Dan would be there, looking wounded, in that bar. She found she could think of the handsome bar owner in a more balanced way, without the angst of the unspoken crush that had haunted her until now.

Owen's expression brightened.

"That sounds great, May. A - a friendly drink."

"Exactly," she nodded. "A friendly drink."

She stood up, feeling comforted and encouraged that things were back to being the same between them.

The same, and yet different.

A door had been opened.

There was no rush. There was lots of time. Things were nice the way they were. In a small town, it was good that things stayed the same. But at any time she wanted, May knew she could take a step through that door. And maybe it would be a good decision.

Maybe it would lead to better things.

She headed out with Owen, walking beside him and feeling happy, and as they reached the main street, her phone began ringing.

It was Kerry, and she felt another surge of worry as she thought about the wedding, and what she might have to face.

"Hey, sis!" Kerry sounded bright and breezy. "Just got in. Brandon will be back in a few minutes from work, so I thought I'd give you a call and have a quick chat about the wedding."

"Yes?" May said. She didn't like the tone of Kerry's voice at all.

"There's a big decision that I haven't told you about yet. Maid of honor."

May swallowed hard. This was it. The moment where her sister would say she was going to give her the task, and while May would be truly honored, she would then want to explode from the stress and the time demands this job would bring.

"Yes?" she asked.

"I don't want to disappoint you. But my friend from school, Helena Jones, has been in touch a few times over the past weeks, and she's been so super-helpful and reminded me about our friendship. Plus, she'd gone through a tough time recently herself. So I thought I'd ask her to be the maid of honor, and I wanted to check with you that you won't be hurt, or mad at me."

May felt relief cascade through her. This was the right choice for everyone.

"I'm not hurt or mad at all. I think that's a very good idea and it will be wonderful for Helena. I'll be a bridesmaid," she smiled.

"For sure. My most special bridesmaid! I just wish Lauren could be one, too."

It was rarely that Kerry spoke about Lauren, but in that moment, May realized that didn't mean her sister didn't think about her. There was a wealth of emotion in her voice.

And it gave May the courage to tell her what she hadn't yet.

"I've reopened that case. I'm relooking at things, trying to find out more," she said.

"You are?" Kerry sounded surprised and intrigued.

"I found something I didn't know was there. A key, with a plastic label. There's writing on it that's too old and smudged to read. I don't know where it is from."

"A key? I also knew nothing about a key," Kerry said.

"I was wondering something."

"Yeah? What?"

"Could you take a look at it? Maybe you can tell where it's from, or there's a software program that can figure out the text on the label?"

Kerry was silent a while. May got the sense this was a big deal for her. A bigger deal than she'd expected.

"I'd love to help," she said. "Send the key, or a picture of it, and I'll take a look and see what I can do."

"Thanks, sis," May said.

"But May," Kerry hesitated.

"What?" she asked. There was something strange in her sister's tone.

"You need to be careful," Kerry warned.

"Why?" May asked.

"Because evidence like this, that wasn't correctly recorded, means something."

"What does it mean?" Now a chill went down May's spine.

"I don't know. But it's very disturbing. There should have been no missing evidence. No mistakes. If there is, it's a sign that someone was able to interfere in the case at some point. This is a small town. People know what's going on, more than you think they do. If you're opening the case and investigating, I'm telling you, be careful. Because if someone thought they'd managed to hide something back then, they're going to do whatever it takes to keep it hidden. Watch your back, is what I'm saying."

"I will." May shivered. "And thank you – for the favor, and the warning."

She cut the call and put her phone away, walking in step with Owen as they approached the bar.

She was unsettled by what Kerry had said, but felt even more determined to unlock the secret behind Lauren's disappearance.

Even if it ended up putting her in personal danger.

NOW AVAILABLE!

NEVER HIDE
(A May Moore Suspense Thriller—Book 4)

From #1 bestselling mystery and suspense author Blake Pierce comes a gripping new series: May Moore, 29, an average Midwestern woman and deputy sheriff, has always lived in the shadow of her older, brilliant FBI agent sister. Yet the sisters are united by the cold case of their missing younger sister—and when a new serial killer strikes in May's quiet, Minnesota lakeside town, it is May's turn to prove herself, to try to outshine her sister and the FBI, and, in this action-packed thriller, to outwit and hunt down a diabolical killer before he strikes again.

"A masterpiece of thriller and mystery."
—Books and Movie Reviews, Roberto Mattos (re Once Gone)

A body is found floating peacefully in the lake in May's hometown, and soon, more begin to appear. This body seems too peaceful, the murder too eerily calm.

Can May enter this killer's mind and crack the case before he claims his next victim?

A page-turning and harrowing crime thriller featuring a brilliant and tortured Deputy Sheriff, the MAY MOORE series is a riveting mystery, packed with non-stop action, suspense, jaw-dropping twists, and driven by a breakneck pace that will keep you flipping pages late into the night.

Books #5 and #6 in the series—NEVER FORGIVE and NEVER AGAIN—are also available!

Blake Pierce

Blake Pierce is the USA Today bestselling author of the RILEY PAGE mystery series, which includes seventeen books. Blake Pierce is also the author of the MACKENZIE WHITE mystery series, comprising fourteen books; of the AVERY BLACK mystery series, comprising six books; of the KERI LOCKE mystery series, comprising five books; of the MAKING OF RILEY PAIGE mystery series, comprising six books; of the KATE WISE mystery series, comprising seven books; of the CHLOE FINE psychological suspense mystery, comprising six books; of the JESSE HUNT psychological suspense thriller series, comprising twenty four books; of the AU PAIR psychological suspense thriller series, comprising three books; of the ZOE PRIME mystery series, comprising six books; of the ADELE SHARP mystery series, comprising fifteen books, of the EUROPEAN VOYAGE cozy mystery series, comprising four books; of the new LAURA FROST FBI suspense thriller, comprising nine books (and counting); of the new ELLA DARK FBI suspense thriller, comprising eleven books (and counting); of the A YEAR IN EUROPE cozy mystery series, comprising nine books, of the AVA GOLD mystery series, comprising six books (and counting); of the RACHEL GIFT mystery series, comprising eight books (and counting); of the VALERIE LAW mystery series, comprising nine books (and counting); of the PAIGE KING mystery series, comprising six books (and counting); of the MAY MOORE mystery series, comprising six books (and counting); and the CORA SHIELDS mystery series, comprising three books (and counting).

An avid reader and lifelong fan of the mystery and thriller genres, Blake loves to hear from you, so please feel free to visit www.blakepierceauthor.com to learn more and stay in touch.

BOOKS BY BLAKE PIERCE

CORA SHIELDS MYSTERY SERIES
UNDONE (Book #1)
UNWANTED (Book #2)
UNHINGED (Book #3)

MAY MOORE SUSPENSE THRILLER
NEVER RUN (Book #1)
NEVER TELL (Book #2)
NEVER LIVE (Book #3)
NEVER HIDE (Book #4)
NEVER FORGIVE (Book #5)
NEVER AGAIN (Book #6)

PAIGE KING MYSTERY SERIES
THE GIRL HE PINED (Book #1)
THE GIRL HE CHOSE (Book #2)
THE GIRL HE TOOK (Book #3)
THE GIRL HE WISHED (Book #4)
THE GIRL HE CROWNED (Book #5)
THE GIRL HE WATCHED (Book #6)

VALERIE LAW MYSTERY SERIES
NO MERCY (Book #1)
NO PITY (Book #2)
NO FEAR (Book #3)
NO SLEEP (Book #4)
NO QUARTER (Book #5)
NO CHANCE (Book #6)
NO REFUGE (Book #7)
NO GRACE (Book #8)
NO ESCAPE (Book #9)

RACHEL GIFT MYSTERY SERIES
HER LAST WISH (Book #1)
HER LAST CHANCE (Book #2)

HER LAST HOPE (Book #3)
HER LAST FEAR (Book #4)
HER LAST CHOICE (Book #5)
HER LAST BREATH (Book #6)
HER LAST MISTAKE (Book #7)
HER LAST DESIRE (Book #8)

AVA GOLD MYSTERY SERIES
CITY OF PREY (Book #1)
CITY OF FEAR (Book #2)
CITY OF BONES (Book #3)
CITY OF GHOSTS (Book #4)
CITY OF DEATH (Book #5)
CITY OF VICE (Book #6)

A YEAR IN EUROPE
A MURDER IN PARIS (Book #1)
DEATH IN FLORENCE (Book #2)
VENGEANCE IN VIENNA (Book #3)
A FATALITY IN SPAIN (Book #4)

ELLA DARK FBI SUSPENSE THRILLER
GIRL, ALONE (Book #1)
GIRL, TAKEN (Book #2)
GIRL, HUNTED (Book #3)
GIRL, SILENCED (Book #4)
GIRL, VANISHED (Book 5)
GIRL ERASED (Book #6)
GIRL, FORSAKEN (Book #7)
GIRL, TRAPPED (Book #8)
GIRL, EXPENDABLE (Book #9)
GIRL, ESCAPED (Book #10)
GIRL, HIS (Book #11)

LAURA FROST FBI SUSPENSE THRILLER
ALREADY GONE (Book #1)
ALREADY SEEN (Book #2)
ALREADY TRAPPED (Book #3)
ALREADY MISSING (Book #4)
ALREADY DEAD (Book #5)

ALREADY TAKEN (Book #6)
ALREADY CHOSEN (Book #7)
ALREADY LOST (Book #8)
ALREADY HIS (Book #9)

EUROPEAN VOYAGE COZY MYSTERY SERIES
MURDER (AND BAKLAVA) (Book #1)
DEATH (AND APPLE STRUDEL) (Book #2)
CRIME (AND LAGER) (Book #3)
MISFORTUNE (AND GOUDA) (Book #4)
CALAMITY (AND A DANISH) (Book #5)
MAYHEM (AND HERRING) (Book #6)

ADELE SHARP MYSTERY SERIES
LEFT TO DIE (Book #1)
LEFT TO RUN (Book #2)
LEFT TO HIDE (Book #3)
LEFT TO KILL (Book #4)
LEFT TO MURDER (Book #5)
LEFT TO ENVY (Book #6)
LEFT TO LAPSE (Book #7)
LEFT TO VANISH (Book #8)
LEFT TO HUNT (Book #9)
LEFT TO FEAR (Book #10)
LEFT TO PREY (Book #11)
LEFT TO LURE (Book #12)
LEFT TO CRAVE (Book #13)
LEFT TO LOATHE (Book #14)
LEFT TO HARM (Book #15)

THE AU PAIR SERIES
ALMOST GONE (Book#1)
ALMOST LOST (Book #2)
ALMOST DEAD (Book #3)

ZOE PRIME MYSTERY SERIES
FACE OF DEATH (Book#1)
FACE OF MURDER (Book #2)
FACE OF FEAR (Book #3)
FACE OF MADNESS (Book #4)

FACE OF FURY (Book #5)
FACE OF DARKNESS (Book #6)

A JESSIE HUNT PSYCHOLOGICAL SUSPENSE SERIES
THE PERFECT WIFE (Book #1)
THE PERFECT BLOCK (Book #2)
THE PERFECT HOUSE (Book #3)
THE PERFECT SMILE (Book #4)
THE PERFECT LIE (Book #5)
THE PERFECT LOOK (Book #6)
THE PERFECT AFFAIR (Book #7)
THE PERFECT ALIBI (Book #8)
THE PERFECT NEIGHBOR (Book #9)
THE PERFECT DISGUISE (Book #10)
THE PERFECT SECRET (Book #11)
THE PERFECT FAÇADE (Book #12)
THE PERFECT IMPRESSION (Book #13)
THE PERFECT DECEIT (Book #14)
THE PERFECT MISTRESS (Book #15)
THE PERFECT IMAGE (Book #16)
THE PERFECT VEIL (Book #17)
THE PERFECT INDISCRETION (Book #18)
THE PERFECT RUMOR (Book #19)
THE PERFECT COUPLE (Book #20)
THE PERFECT MURDER (Book #21)
THE PERFECT HUSBAND (Book #22)
THE PERFECT SCANDAL (Book #23)
THE PERFECT MASK (Book #24)

CHLOE FINE PSYCHOLOGICAL SUSPENSE SERIES
NEXT DOOR (Book #1)
A NEIGHBOR'S LIE (Book #2)
CUL DE SAC (Book #3)
SILENT NEIGHBOR (Book #4)
HOMECOMING (Book #5)
TINTED WINDOWS (Book #6)

KATE WISE MYSTERY SERIES
IF SHE KNEW (Book #1)

IF SHE SAW (Book #2)
IF SHE RAN (Book #3)
IF SHE HID (Book #4)
IF SHE FLED (Book #5)
IF SHE FEARED (Book #6)
IF SHE HEARD (Book #7)

THE MAKING OF RILEY PAIGE SERIES
WATCHING (Book #1)
WAITING (Book #2)
LURING (Book #3)
TAKING (Book #4)
STALKING (Book #5)
KILLING (Book #6)

RILEY PAIGE MYSTERY SERIES
ONCE GONE (Book #1)
ONCE TAKEN (Book #2)
ONCE CRAVED (Book #3)
ONCE LURED (Book #4)
ONCE HUNTED (Book #5)
ONCE PINED (Book #6)
ONCE FORSAKEN (Book #7)
ONCE COLD (Book #8)
ONCE STALKED (Book #9)
ONCE LOST (Book #10)
ONCE BURIED (Book #11)
ONCE BOUND (Book #12)
ONCE TRAPPED (Book #13)
ONCE DORMANT (Book #14)
ONCE SHUNNED (Book #15)
ONCE MISSED (Book #16)
ONCE CHOSEN (Book #17)

MACKENZIE WHITE MYSTERY SERIES
BEFORE HE KILLS (Book #1)
BEFORE HE SEES (Book #2)
BEFORE HE COVETS (Book #3)
BEFORE HE TAKES (Book #4)
BEFORE HE NEEDS (Book #5)

BEFORE HE FEELS (Book #6)
BEFORE HE SINS (Book #7)
BEFORE HE HUNTS (Book #8)
BEFORE HE PREYS (Book #9)
BEFORE HE LONGS (Book #10)
BEFORE HE LAPSES (Book #11)
BEFORE HE ENVIES (Book #12)
BEFORE HE STALKS (Book #13)
BEFORE HE HARMS (Book #14)

AVERY BLACK MYSTERY SERIES
CAUSE TO KILL (Book #1)
CAUSE TO RUN (Book #2)
CAUSE TO HIDE (Book #3)
CAUSE TO FEAR (Book #4)
CAUSE TO SAVE (Book #5)
CAUSE TO DREAD (Book #6)

KERI LOCKE MYSTERY SERIES
A TRACE OF DEATH (Book #1)
A TRACE OF MURDER (Book #2)
A TRACE OF VICE (Book #3)
A TRACE OF CRIME (Book #4)
A TRACE OF HOPE (Book #5)